Was this really happening?

Natalie moved the Brailler to one side of her desk. Her mind drifted. *Learning Braille would be admitting that you have a serious vision problem. . . .* Meredith's chirpy voice echoed: You'll see. . . . Natalie's cranky reply haunted: But I won't see!

Those Braille cells had staked out a spot in her brain and were doing calisthenics. Natalie couldn't get them out of her head now. Thank goodness there were only two more days until she could get on a bus and go home for the weekend. She wanted to sleep in her own bed, cook with her mother, get her hands on the goats, and tell Meredith so many things: how sorry she was about the phone call, how Eve had no concept of color and memorized her clothes by the way they felt, how much she hated the cane—and maybe—maybe she would confide in Meredith—about how much she had changed in the past three weeks, ever since the last visit with Dr. Rose. No one else knew how scared she was, underneath.

Would Meredith be able to help her? Would she even want to help her? Or would confiding her fear simply scare away her friends? They could be fluky, especially Coralee and Suzanne. Probably best not to let any of them in on it, she concluded. They wouldn't be able to deal with it.

God knows those weren't the biggest questions either, because deep, deep down in her core, Natalie wondered if she would be able to deal with it, too.

OTHER BOOKS YOU MAY ENJOY

PRISCILLA CUMMINGS

BLIND SIDED

PUFFIN BOOKS
An Imprint of Penguin Group (USA) Inc.

PUFFIN BOOKS

Published by the Penguin Group

Penguin Young Readers Group, 345 Hudson Street, New York, New York 10014, U.S.A.

Penguin Group (Canada), 90 Eglinton Avenue East, Suite 700, Toronto, Ontario, Canada M4P 2Y3
(a division of Pearson Penguin Canada Inc.)

Penguin Books Ltd, 80 Strand, London WC2R 0RL, England

Penguin Ireland, 25 St Stephen's Green, Dublin 2, Ireland (a division of Penguin Books Ltd)

Penguin Group (Australia), 250 Camberwell Road, Camberwell, Victoria 3124, Australia
(a division of Pearson Australia Group Pty Ltd)

Penguin Books India Pvt Ltd, 11 Community Centre, Panchsheel Park, New Delhi - 110 017, India

Penguin Group (NZ), 67 Apollo Drive, Rosedale, Auckland 0632, New Zealand
(a division of Pearson New Zealand Ltd.)

Penguin Books (South Africa) (Pty) Ltd, 24 Sturdee Avenue,
Rosebank, Johannesburg 2196, South Africa

Registered Offices: Penguin Books Ltd, 80 Strand, London WC2R 0RL, England

First published in the United States of America by Dutton Children's Books,
a division of Penguin Young Readers Group, 2010
Published by Puffin Books, a division of Penguin Young Readers Group, 2011

7 9 10 8

THE LIBRARY OF CONGRESS HAS CATALOGED THE DUTTON'S CHILDREN'S BOOKS EDITION AS FOLLOWS:

Cummings, Priscilla, date.

Blindsided / by Priscilla Cummings

p. cm.

Summary: After years of failing eyesight, fourteen-year-old Natalie reluctantly enters
a school for the blind, where in spite of her initial resistance she learns the skills
that will help her survive in the sighted world.

ISBN 978-0-525-42161-0 (hc)

[1. Blind—Fiction. 2. People with disabilities—Fiction. 3. Schools—Fiction. 4. Maryland—Fiction.]
I. Title.

PZ7.C9149Bl 2010

[Fic]—dc22

2009025092

Puffin Books ISBN 978-0-14-241902-1

Designed by Irene Vandervoort
Set in Minion

Printed in the United States of America

*This book is dedicated to all the blind teenagers—and adults—
who spoke with me over many months.
Whether it was a personal conversation, an e-mail exchange,
or a telephone call, I will never forget how much you opened
your hearts so that I could see. . . .*

ACKNOWLEDGMENTS

I thank the teachers, staff, and administrators at the Maryland School for the Blind in Baltimore, Maryland, for the generous access the school community provided me during an entire academic year. But I especially thank the students. Out of concerns for privacy, I am not going to thank each student individually. But I could not have written this story without their help in sharing with me their personal stories, their successes and fears—and their abundant humor. My gratitude to them, and my respect for them, is enormous.

I thank instructors, staff, and young people participating in programs at the National Federation of the Blind in Baltimore, and employees of Blind Industries, State of Maryland (BISM).

I am grateful to David Faucheux for his many e-mails from Louisiana; to Melissa Sheeder, a student at Catonsville Community College; and to Danielle Shives, a senior at Frostburg University.

Special thanks to Dr. William F. Bruther, my own ophthalmologist in Annapolis, who kindly provided many detailed explanations of issues related to vision and workings of the eye. Thanks also to Dr. Nicole Love, an ophthalmologist who provides care throughout Maryland to individuals with low vision, including to students at the Maryland School for the Blind; and Dr. Neil R. Miller, professor and chairman of the neuro-ophthalmology unit, Wilmer Eye Institute at Johns Hopkins Hospital in Baltimore.

I appreciate the help given by friends John, Karen, and Sophie Bambacus. And I thank Andrea and Matt Cedro of Firefly Farms,

Ron and Virginia Weimer, and Joy Eliassen for an education in goat farming.

Thanks go to my friend and nursing consultant, Carol Stewart, and her literary son, Charlie.

As always, I am grateful for the support of my family—my husband, John; my children, William and Hannah; as well as my insightful agent, Ann Tobias; and my patient editor, Rosanne Lauer.

I want to acknowledge the book *Safe Without Sight* by Wendy David, Ph.D., Kerry Kollmar, and Scott McCall. And I thank the National Braille Press, Boston, Massachusetts, for allowing me to quote from the book.

Last but not least, a special, heartfelt thanks to teacher Beth Ann Krug, who prompted this story, some years ago now, by encouraging Travis to show me the poem he had written about being blind.

"The best and most beautiful things in the world cannot be seen, or even touched—they must be felt with the heart."

—HELEN KELLER

CONTENTS

A REAL NUISANCE

Like so many of Natalie's early memories, this one is full of color: the fresh yellow straw, the red blood that was pooling way too fast, the silver bucket kicked aside, the damp, quivering brown fur.

"Hurry, Natty, but don't slip and fall!" her father ordered as he placed the towel-wrapped newborn in Natalie's waiting arms. "I'm going to try to save the twin."

Natalie's moist and frightened eyes widened. "What about Daisy?"

"I'll do what I can," he said. Then he touched her arm and reminded her quickly, but calmly, "And I'll do what I have to do."

Natalie swallowed hard and nodded.

"Now you go on and do what *you* have to do. Do you understand?"

"Yes," she replied, her firm response hiding the anxiety that prickled up and down her spine. She was eight years old then. What if she messed up?

It was early January, a cold, black night softened only by a slice of pale moonlight reflecting off the crusty snow. Natalie hurriedly picked her way across the frozen yard with the extraordinary bundle in her arms. It was not a good time of year to be born, but sometimes the goats didn't listen to reason—or season.

3

In the house, Natalie held the kid tightly against her bulky parka with one hand while she drew warm water in the deep white porcelain set tub, the one her mother used to wash the milking equipment. Still holding the little goat—she bet it didn't weigh more than six or seven pounds—she scooted to the bathroom and grabbed more clean towels.

If only her mother had known Daisy was close to delivering, she wouldn't have gone to the town meeting. She'd be there, in the house, doing all these things with confident, experienced hands. Daisy was her mother's favorite. She was the first dairy goat they ever owned, the reason they decided to buy more goats and start the farm. Her mother would be devastated if something happened to Daisy, or any of her babies.

Natalie rushed back into the kitchen, threw the towels on the table, and then swung open the freezer compartment to the refrigerator, plucking a plastic container of colostrum from the side shelf. Mother goat's first milk. A good thing they kept some for emergencies. The kid would need it to survive. One-handed because she was still holding the baby, Natalie set the double boiler on the stove. She filled the bottom pot with water, set the colostrum in a second, smaller pan, and nestled it on top of the larger pot before turning on the heat. The gas flame rose with a *whoosh*. Natalie turned it way down; the precious liquid needed to warm slowly so it wouldn't turn into pudding.

Next, she returned to the set tub and turned off the water. "Okay, here we go," she murmured as she carefully unpeeled the soiled towel, letting it fall on the floor, and lowered the shivering kid with both hands into the warm water. Natalie still had her coat on because she couldn't take the time to remove it, and the bottoms of her sleeves got soaked. "Easy, now. That's it." The goat was so small that, with Natalie's support, it stood in the tub with water up to its neck. An exact miniature of its mother, the kid was solid brown except for a little white star on its forehead—and, of course, the long droopy ears. It was so new, so cold, and so weak, it didn't protest at all, but let Natalie bathe and wipe it clean. She paid special attention to those big ears that distinguished Nubians. She even remembered to check its eyes, to be sure no eyelashes were turned under.

Wow. Could she see that well then, to have done that? To have actually seen the kid's eyelashes?

Seated, finally, in a kitchen chair, with the tiny goat dry and wrapped in a fresh towel, Natalie offered the warmed colostrum in a baby bottle. Confused at first, the kid caught on quickly and eagerly sucked down the nourishment. Natalie took in a full breath, then let it out and smiled, feeling her body relax with relief. As she gazed upon the helpless creature in her lap, her heart filled with love while her mind raced ahead to what she needed to do next: dip the kid's umbilical cord in iodine soon—real soon—and find a heat lamp for the stall so Daisy and her babies would be warm.

She had plowed through her anxieties and did what needed to be done. And yet, the peace that flowed from this proud moment was short-lived. Seconds later, a rifle shot rang out from the barn. Natalie stiffened and sat up. Tears sprang into her eyes as she hugged the now-orphaned goat and bent to kiss its head, imploring it not to worry, and promising that she would always be there to take care of it.

A long, hard winter followed and, much to Natalie's delight, they had no choice but to let the kid stay inside with them. Natalie fixed its bottle and fed it in the morning before school, then again when she came home, and once more before bed. On the fifth day of its life, while it wriggled like crazy, Natalie held the little goat tight on her lap while her father used a hot debudding iron to burn out the two nubs on its head where horns had started to emerge. Natalie knew it was necessary; dairy goats with horns could seriously hurt one another. Still, a minute turned into eternity while the sizzling iron created tiny, terrible wisps of smoke. When it was over, relief once again. Natalie had a warm bottle waiting to comfort her baby.

The orphaned kid quickly outgrew the wooden crate Natalie's father had hauled in, and soon it was moved into a newspaper-lined playpen by the woodstove. Natalie and her best friend, Meredith, took the goat upstairs to Natalie's room where they dressed it in baby clothes. In her snapshot memory, Natalie could still see the bright yellow bonnet edged with white lace and a pink sweater with green turtle buttons. The girls laughed themselves silly watching the kid cavort happily with its bonnet brim flapping and its tiny hooves clicking like small tap shoes across the channels of wood floor in between rugs.

The goat, of course, thought Natalie was its mother and followed her everywhere, an endearing but sometimes problematic situation. Hence, the name: Nuisance. In some ways, Nuisance was the little brother or sister Natalie never had. Everyone in the family developed an enormous soft spot for the little goat and forgave it some awfully bad habits, such as munching on the houseplants and sampling everything it found in the wastebasket. The kid was so spoiled, it even rode, buckled into a seat, with the O'Reillys in their van. Natalie told the goat her deepest secrets, combed its short brown hair with a doll's brush, and lovingly stroked its Roman nose and long ears hundreds of times. If her parents had let her, Natalie would have allowed the goat to sleep in her bed, or to stand, with a bib tied on, atop a chair beside her at the dinner table.

———

As winter turned to spring, Nuisance grew and the little goat's world expanded—to the yard, to the barn, and finally, the wide green pastures filled with other goats. But Natalie's world started to shrink, and fade.

The color is gone from these memories. They are all in black and white: Natalie, colliding with a beam in the hayloft and nearly knocking herself out; tripping, falling, and splitting open her lip in the grocery store parking lot; tumbling down the basement stairs and winding up with a dozen bruises and a huge, sore egg on her forehead.

It's not that Natalie suddenly couldn't see anything; she just couldn't see as much. The outer edges of her field of vision—the periphery—were suddenly blurry. So she missed seeing important parts of her world, such as the white-painted asphalt curb in the parking lot and the edge of the top stair to the basement. As she explained it to her younger cousin: "Pretend your hands are binoculars, Florie. Roll your fingers. Now. Can you see me?" The little girl had nodded. "Yeah, I can see—but only parts of you. It's like the world got shrinked." And that was it exactly, Natalie had thought: *It's like the world got shrinked.* She didn't always have the complete picture right off, but with a little time she could piece things together.

Please don't take any more away. Please. I already have to wear a hat all the time—I'm keeping the bright light out. And I do those eyedrops twice a day. Isn't that enough?

Reading became a struggle, too. Natalie was given special equipment that she had to push from the library to her classroom on a rolling cart. She had always been a little small for her age and it was a lot of work maneuvering that big cart around, but it enabled her to enlarge and darken the letters in her textbooks so that she could see them more easily.

Her confidential talks with Nuisance began to sound like prayers: *I'm scared, but I don't want anyone to know, not Mom and Dad, and not even Meredith, 'cause I don't want them to worry and look at me like I'm different. That's why I have to work so hard at school to be perfect, to make up for some of the dumb things I do. I just can't help it. Like bumping into people when I'm pushing the cart, or tripping over Stephen Handley, who was sitting in the hall yesterday. I broke his pencil and ripped my favorite black pants. It was so embarrassing. . . .*

When she started middle school, the cart simply stayed in the library and with classes in several different locations every day, life became far more complicated. Meredith, and sometimes Coralee and Suzanne, knew Natalie was having trouble and helped guide her. But while Natalie could always count on Meredith, the other girls were hit and miss, which sometimes left Natalie stranded, and embarrassingly late to class. Twice—and this was especially humiliating—she even walked into the wrong room and had to be directed out by the teacher, while the students stifled chuckles in the background.

Never was that going to happen again, Natalie swore to herself. That's when she started counting. *Forty-two steps between Mr. Hewitt's ancient history class and the doors to downstairs . . . six steps to the water fountain . . . fourteen steps to the girls' room . . .*

"We have to do something," Natalie's mother insisted after dinner one evening when Natalie was nearing the end of eighth grade. She stacked the dinner dishes on the counter and sat down again at the table. "Dr. Rose says her eyesight is getting worse, not better."

"What do you suggest?" Natalie's father asked. He had pliers and was trying to fix the buckle on a goat halter.

"Well, I had a note from school, from this woman who helps Natalie prepare homework and take notes."

Her father looked up. "What woman?"

"What's her name, Natalie?"

Natalie picked at a hangnail on her thumb. "Mrs. Russell," she replied glumly. "She's the vision teacher. She travels around to all the schools."

"Yes. Mrs. Russell. A nice woman," Natalie's mother noted. "She's been very helpful. She's suggesting that Natalie learn Braille."

"Braille?!" That certainly got her father's full attention. Natalie heard the clink of the buckle as he set the halter on the table. "What are you talking about, Jean? Natalie doesn't need to learn Braille! She's getting straight A's in school! She's writing beautiful poetry about the mountains. She babysits. She helps me in the barn—"

"No one is saying Natalie isn't bright or capable, Frank!" her mother interjected. "Mrs. Russell is simply looking down the road—"

"Yeah, well, tell Mrs. Russell to look *up* instead of down." He sounded angry. Exactly how Natalie felt, too. No way did she want to learn Braille. That was for blind people. No way was she going there!

And yet, deep down inside, Natalie worried that her mother was right. So she remained silent, torn between her mother's frightening practicality and her father's shuttered and emotional defense.

Natalie's mother sighed and got up to wash the dishes. Her father stood and pushed his chair in. Natalie asked if she could be excused to go do her homework, but paused in the next room to listen.

"Don't rush into things, Jean," her father added, quietly, before he walked out the door. "That's all I'm saying. Let's be optimistic. Give Natty some time. Her eyes will get better."

Memories fade to gray after that because nothing was very clear anymore. The only thing for certain was that Natalie's eyes were not getting better. The summer before she started high school, there was even a panic when the pressure in her eyes increased so much that more surgery had to be scheduled. It would be the seventh time Natalie had been in the operating room for her eyes.

When will it end? Why is this happening to me?

Her father told her not to worry, that the next surgery could be the turning point. One day, he even brought home a small pink stone—from the feed store of all places—that had the word HOPE etched into it. "They had these in a little bowl on the counter," he said, pressing it into her hand. "Keep it in your pocket, Natty Bean. Don't ever forget there's always hope." And Natalie had hugged her dad, who, in his worn denim jacket, smelled just like a sack of grain.

"Is there something you would like to do?" her mother suddenly asked two weeks before the scheduled operation. "Something you've always wanted to *see*, Natalie?"

What? Is Mom afraid I'll come out of surgery with no sight at all?

"The ocean," Natalie blurted. A mistake. A huge mistake because that trip to the beach was a disaster. Her father was bored, just sitting under an umbrella all day, and he worried about the goats the whole time. Her mother, who had had some skin cancer on her nose, had to sit in the shade, covered up almost the whole time. She didn't even want to take a long walk. And then the one time Natalie summoned her courage to go out in the ocean a big wave knocked her down and scared her half to death. No. They never should have gone.

Fortunately, the surgery was successful. The pressure went down and Natalie's vision did not get worse.

But it didn't get better either.

A year later, just before her sophomore year began, Natalie was told by her eye doctor to prepare for the worst and, although they disagreed at first, her parents decided to send her to a special school where she could learn the skills she needed to cope with vision loss. On the last morning she was home, Natalie finished packing her suitcase and carried it downstairs, dropping it heavily by the front door. She did not want to be leaving for this special school hundreds of miles away.

Without saying anything to her mother, Natalie took a dog biscuit and went to the barn to say good-bye to Nuisance. It was early, just after dawn, and the fog was lifting. Natalie could feel the moisture on her face and hands. She still had a small circle of vision, but just to be sure, as always, she counted the fifty-eight steps from the back kitchen door to the barn. The feral cat that waited for a pan of leftover milk every morning meowed at Natalie from its post on the cement stoop near the milking parlor. Yellow light spilled from a row of square glass panes. On the other side of the wall, Natalie's father and Uncle Jack were already busy. Milking machines hummed and pails clanged.

Inside the barn, the smell of fresh hay from the loft above and the pungent odor of manure from the pens mixed and surrounded her. The goats moved around restlessly in their pens, eager to be milked and get their morning portion of grain.

"Hey, Nuisance!" she called sweetly, standing at the enclosure where her goat shared quarters with twelve other Nubians. "Nuisy Juicy!"

Instantly, several goats rushed to where she stood, greeting Natalie with a chorus of *wahhhhhhh* and competing for her attention. One of them stood up against the rails and leaned over to tug on her sweater. Another nibbled at her fingers.

"Stop!" she had to tell them, although not without a smile. When she moved her hand to push away the biggest aggressor, another goat stole the biscuit. Was it Nuisance? Her heart dropped; she couldn't be sure. A blur of brown and white, all of them. Natalie couldn't see well enough to tell them apart anymore.

"I'll be back," she promised the goats, hoping Nuisance heard. "I'll be back," she repeated, whispering, "and everything will be okay."

She believed it.

DAY ONE

From the very first day, Natalie wanted all the students at her new school to know she was *not* like them—and never would be. It's not that she was being mean. She just wanted to establish some boundaries.

So when she moved into her small, spare dormitory room, Natalie immediately planted a small forest of framed pictures on her bureau: Natalie, candle in hand, with her mom and dad the evening she was inducted into the National Honor Society; Natalie and Meredith, dressed like cats for Spirit Day—fuzzy ears glued to headbands, stuffed black panty hose for tails, whiskers painted on pale cheeks with eyeliner. There was the photograph—the one that ran in the newspaper—of Natalie campaigning door-to-door with Professor Brodsky from the nearby college, a candidate for state senator. And there was the rhinestone-studded frame surrounding Natalie, light brown bangs brushing her eyebrows, a smile dimpling her lightly freckled cheeks, as she cuddled, head to head, with floppy-eared Nuisance.

The pictures confirmed what Natalie couldn't exactly say out loud: *I am a normal person. An excellent student with big dreams. A typical teenager with friends who are cool—and normal like me.*

While her mother settled a suitcase on the extra bed (thank

God there was not a roommate, Natalie thought) and zipped it open to unpack, Natalie rushed to tape a Western Allegany High School pennant to the bland, beige wall over her bed. Then she filled the four drawers of her single bureau with brown sweatshirts, sweatpants, T-shirts, and shorts that all bore the same orange letters and snarling cougar, her high school's mascot. A brown and orange cougar mug was placed in a prominent spot on her desk. And a brown and orange cougar baseball cap was on her head at all times.

Lest they think otherwise, Natalie wanted to be sure all the students knew that she was temporary, here only long enough to learn what she needed—just in case—whereupon she would return to finish high school with her friends. "An insurance policy," her father called it the night before when Natalie was feeling down and wouldn't eat dinner. Her mother had already left the room, her own meal barely touched. Natalie heard the kitchen door close, and then the sound of her mother's footsteps down the back stairs as a current of cool air seeped into the kitchen, stirring the pained silence. Natalie's father reached across the table to cover Natalie's hand with his own large one. "Don't blame your mother," he said. "Just go and learn everything you have to, Nat, and hope you never need it."

Hope, yes. That was the bedrock of her soul, wasn't it? She squeezed the pink stone in her pocket and ran her thumb over the engraved letters.

"Hey there!" a voice startled Natalie. She whirled around to see a girl in a wheelchair parked in the doorway of her dorm room. "Hi, I'm Paula," the girl said.

"Oh—hi," Natalie replied cautiously. She noticed the girl's head was bobbing around in a strange way.

"I heard you were new." Paula smiled. "I just wanted to say 'welcome.'"

Not long afterward, a girl dressed all in black wandered over from the room across the hall and leaned against the same doorway. "Yeah. So my name's Serena. If you need anything let me know."

And it hit Natalie with a thud. *Duh.* She felt so stupid. All the work she'd done to decorate the room in a way that identified and protected her was for no one's benefit other than her own. Not a single other student could appreciate it. Because none of them could see.

A PARALLEL UNIVERSE

Natalie didn't think she'd ever fall asleep that first night, but she must have because in the morning, she awakened with a start. The ocean dream again. A nightmare actually, with water and darkness engulfing her. Why did it haunt her this way? Disoriented, her heart pounding, she scrambled to turn on the light. Instead, her fingers bumped into the smooth, cold base of the new lamp on her desk at school, and the reality of where she was washed over her like a huge, stomach-churning wave of nausea.

A strange institutional hum came from somewhere outside the room. Natalie rolled over and pulled the blankets over her head. How long did she lie there? Did she fall back asleep? A knock at the door awakened her a second time.

"Natalie, do you need some help this morning?" The voice was an older woman's, possibly the dorm counselor she'd met the day before.

Natalie whipped the blanket away from her face. "No!" she called out. "No, thank you!" Accepting help meant she needed assistance and that would be admitting to a problem. "I'm okay!" she added before pulling the covers back over her head.

"All right, hon. Just to let you know it's seven o'clock. We'll gather in the lobby to go to breakfast in half an hour."

She could stay where she was, Natalie thought, gripping the edge of the blanket. Just stay in bed, hiding out. But there were no locks on the door, so they would come in, wouldn't they? They would force her to go to class, then she'd be embarrassed and they would call her parents and her mother would get all upset and ask Natalie if she'd already forgotten everything they talked about. *What's going on?* If her mother got upset, then her father would get upset, too. *We shouldn't have forced her to go, Jean. . . . Stop it, Frank! You know she needed to do this!* And everything would get off to a really bad start. Natalie did not want things to get off to a bad start.

Sighing, she pushed the covers off and forced herself to sit up. She reached for the tinted eyeglasses she had left on the desk beside her and groaned when she saw again with her small circle of vision how she was awash in all that beige—walls, floors, doors. The bathroom was ten steps to the right of the small shag rug beneath her feet. The tile floor was cold. She winced and walked fast.

Seven o'clock. Her dad would be in the barn milking goats. Her mother would be cleaning up from breakfast, putting a few scraps in the old pie tin for the cat. Natalie wished she could be the one taking the food to the cat; she'd been trying to make friends with it for weeks. Instead, here she was, plucking underwear out of a strange dresser drawer hundreds of miles away.

She felt around and grabbed a pair of Peds, then pushed the top drawer shut. T-shirts were third drawer down, sweatpants in the bottom. She dressed quickly, did her eyedrops, and pulled her straight, shoulder-length hair into a ponytail. Finally, she put on her baseball cap, fishing her ponytail out through the back opening, and found the pink stone, which she'd left beside her hairbrush, and pushed it into the right pocket of her sweatpants.

Pressing the little button on her watch—it was impossible to see those tiny numbers—she held it to her ear and listened: *The time is . . . seven . . . ten . . . A.M.*"

Twenty minutes left. Natalie put her pajamas away, then quickly made up her bed and sat on it, staring at nothing, just using up time, wondering what the day would be like and trying hard not to think of home again.

Twenty-nine steps from Natalie's bedroom to the lobby, with a left-hand turn after eighteen. She had counted the steps last night after the dorm meeting as a kind of backup so she could find her way without asking for help.

"Good morning, Natalie," the counselor greeted her in the dorm lobby where the other girls had gathered. It was a different counselor from the one last night, but Natalie didn't care enough to try to remember their names, or do all the work of moving her head around and mentally piecing together the small bits of vision to see what the person looked like. "We're going to have you do sighted guide with Serena today. You're both in the same classes. Are you familiar with sighted guide?"

Weakly, Natalie nodded. "Yes," she said. Sighted guide meant taking another person's elbow and letting them lead. But she didn't need it. Didn't *want* it would be more to the point. People here would get the wrong idea. Should she speak up?

There wasn't time. The others were on the move, most of the girls swinging canes in front of them. Natalie had to step out of the way.

Serena sidled over to her. "I'm not awake yet," she mumbled. "I'll try not to lead you astray."

Natalie turned to her. "I'm not blind," she blurted.

Serena sniffed. "No," she said, shrugging. "I'm not either."

Natalie frowned. "But—"

"Come on. I need coffee," Serena said.

Confused, Natalie took Serena's left elbow with her right hand, swallowed her pride, and let the girl lead her out the dormitory door and down a cement sidewalk toward the dining hall.

Somehow, Serena knew where they were supposed to sit and threaded their way between tables to the right one. Slowly, other teenagers joined them. Some used canes that they folded and put on the floor, underneath their chairs. A couple mumbled "Good morning," but most simply sat down without a word.

"They're setting a platter of French toast on the table, Natalie. There's also hash browns and eggs. And you can always have cold cereal instead."

"French toast is good," Natalie said. She felt her stomach rumble. She hadn't eaten much dinner the night before after her mother left.

Serena handed her a plate from a stack on the table, then set a container of maple syrup in front of her.

"Do you want coffee?"

"Can I just have water?" Natalie asked.

"Sure." Serena pulled a pitcher of water across the table. "There's a stack of cups right there, in front of you."

Natalie busied herself with breakfast. The French toast was thin and tasted funny, not at all like her mother's. And the maple syrup was the imitation kind with a gummy texture, not like the real stuff they made themselves back home. Natalie ate it all anyway, washing it down with two cups of water.

"So you thought this place was just for the blind?" Serena asked after they'd finished eating. She sipped her coffee and held the mug in her hands. When people stayed in one place long enough, Natalie could get a pretty good look. She noticed how Serena was dressed in black again and that the long-sleeved shirt she wore had holes toward the end of each sleeve where her thumbs popped through.

"I did think this place was for the blind," Natalie replied. "I mean, this is the Baltimore Center for the Blind, isn't it?"

Serena smiled. "Yeah, it is."

"But you can see, too?" Natalie asked.

"Yeah, I can see," Serena replied. She set her coffee down and with one thumb and a forefinger she pulled a few strands of red-streaked raven black hair toward the corner of her mouth while seeming to keep a cool, steady eye on Natalie.

"I can see *some* anyway. But only out of my left eye."

It seemed rude, suddenly, to be asking someone if they could see or not. Natalie shook her head. "I'm sorry, I didn't mean to be nosy—"

"No, no, it's okay. I don't mind. I mean, not everyone talks about why they're here, but it's pretty obvious. Just that some people are more sensitive to it than others. We're not all totally blind, no way."

Serena beckoned for Natalie to come close, then leaned toward her and lowered her voice again behind her hand. "Okay. The kids at our table?"

Natalie glanced around, best she could.

"Right across from you, that guy? The tall one? That's Sheldon," Serena said. "He has Leber's disease, where you lose the central part of your vision, but you can see around the edges. And next to him, that's Jerome—JJ we call him. He's totally blind and has been since he was really little. The other boy who looks Indian—he's new. Arnab. He's cute, isn't he?"

"Arnab, yes. I met him yesterday at a reception," Natalie said, recalling how her mother had introduced them to a couple families, despite Natalie's desire to skip the event. She remembered that Arnab was handsome, even though he held one of his arms across his chest in a funny way. And he spoke so precisely, with an accent. "I am very pleased"—which sounded like plea-said—"to meet you, Natalie." Arnab's mother wore a colorful sari and had leaned toward Natalie, whispering that Arnab lost his sight in an automobile accident. "He is such a smart boy. Such a good boy," she'd murmured softly, before her voice cracked.

"I don't know anything about him, but he must be a brain," Serena said. "I hear he wants to take calculus." Serena's voice grew softer. "Okay. Eve, next to me over here? The girl with the ponytail? She's never had vision. Her little brothers used to steal her food. That's why she's hunched over and has her arm wrapped around her plate. But you can't tell her that no one's going to rip off her food here. I mean, why would we?"

Straightening up, she stopped whispering. "Us kids in the academic program, we're sort of like a parallel universe here. We're in the minority, anyway. There's only, like, twenty-five of us." She ran her index finger in the remaining maple syrup on her plate and licked it, and Natalie could see that the wires in her braces were black, too.

There were only twenty-five of them? Natalie glanced around the large room at the other tables.

"Who else is here then?" Natalie asked.

"A lot of younger kids and—"

A loud wail suddenly pierced the air, interrupting Serena.

"Those kids," Serena said. "Over to your left."

Natalie could see the wheelchairs gathered around several tables. It appeared that most of the kids were strapped into their chairs and were being fed by adult helpers who sat beside them. Now that she focused on it, she could see there was a lot of flailing about going on. And she realized that they were the source of the strange moaning.

"Obviously, eyesight isn't their only problem. I think the state doesn't know what else to do with them," Serena said. "At least that's what I've heard. First time I saw them, I was totally freaked. I thought, 'Ho-*ly*! Is that going to happen to me?' Besides being blind, some of them can't walk or talk or anything,"

"Really?" Natalie couldn't even begin to imagine what kind of life they had.

"You get used to having them here, though."

"Gosh, I feel sorry for them," Natalie said.

"Oh, yeah! Me too!" Serena agreed. "But still, they ought to warn you about it, you know? Anyway, that's why we're, like, in this parallel universe here."

A parallel universe. Natalie tried to look around at the kids in her group. She knew next to nothing about the other students, other than a few first names. Serena, of course. Serena with her black clothes and, Natalie now realized, black nail polish. She was a little pudgy, but she had a round, pretty face and seemed to pride herself on being outspoken. At the first dorm meeting last evening, brief because not all the girls had arrived yet, Serena had been blunt about her feelings on a number of issues: About lights out at 10 P.M.: "That sucks!" About the tight schedule: "Where is my downtime? When will I watch Dr. Phil and Oprah? Y'all are going to stress me out." And with regard to cell phone use only after 8 P.M.: "This is like prison!"

Natalie tried to get a better look at quiet Eve, who had just hooked two fingers over the rim of her glass and, with her other hand, was pouring water from a pitcher into the glass. So that's how they did it, Natalie realized. Somehow, Eve had special permission to keep a bird in her room. Natalie had heard it singing last night. Odd, but it sounded like a red-winged blackbird—was it possible?—which only reminded Natalie of the creek back home.

How fast yesterday's trip had gone, even though it had taken more than five hours for Natalie and her mother to drive across the state from Hawley, in Maryland's western mountains, to Baltimore near the Chesapeake Bay. A black bear had been spotted in the hills that morning, not far from Natalie's home, and her father thought it best to stay back and keep an extra eye on the goats. She and her mother shared tea from a thermos and nibbled on snickerdoodles that Meredith had brought over as a going-away gift. When her mother announced that they had arrived at the school, Natalie didn't want to believe it.

"We're here already?" She sat up as the car slowed for a speed bump. All Natalie could see outside were trees, lots and lots of trees clumped together in a grayish-green cluster. She swallowed hard. A knot had rooted itself in her stomach the moment they turned out of their farm's rutted, dirt driveway, and it had grown with every passing mile. By the time they reached the entrance to the school in Baltimore, the knot had become so large that Natalie could barely breathe.

"Can we go get an iced tea somewhere first?" she had asked. "Couldn't we just drive around the area a little first? Please?"

"It's time," her mother had insisted, her voice calm, but edged with fatigue. "You know it's time. You need to learn these skills."

But it couldn't be time, Natalie thought to herself. New skills would only be necessary if Natalie went blind and that just couldn't happen. Natalie did not want to lose her sight. No way! A world of darkness? A world alone?

"It's going to be all right," her mother reassured her as they continued up the driveway.

But Natalie wasn't so sure. She slid down in the car seat and fixed her narrow gaze outside, saying nothing as her mother drove up the long, shaded entrance to the school.

Because sometimes when you're scared, *really* scared, you just shut up and do what people tell you to do.

ARE THEY KIDDING?

An argument suddenly erupted at the lunch table.

The two boys across from Natalie yelled and pushed away from each other. Natalie tried to recall their names.

"You got to be kidding me, man!" the taller, more slender one yelled. Sheldon, Natalie remembered. That was Sheldon yelling.

"No, I'm not kidding!" the other replied.

"You on a diet, JJ?" Sheldon was asking. "What for?"

JJ was the other boy.

"What you think I'm on a diet for?" JJ retorted, annoyed.

So it wasn't really an argument. Just a loud conversation. Loud teasing. Now that Natalie was getting a better look, she could see that maybe JJ did need to lose some weight. She also noticed he had spilled some ketchup on his shirt. The large red blob and a thin, watery red dribble made it look as though he'd been shot in the chest.

"No seconds this year," JJ told Sheldon. He didn't seem to know about the ketchup stain. "And I'm walking around the track every day."

Sheldon folded his arms on the table and dropped his head on them.

"I am getting a girlfriend this year!" JJ declared.

Sheldon's arms and shoulders shook with laughter.

"What kind of girlfriend will you be wantin' this year?" Serena jumped in, egging him on.

"A big girl," JJ said seriously. "A Christian girl."

"Well, I guess that leaves me out," Serena quipped. "I suppose she has to be a virgin, too."

Sheldon laughed harder and Natalie put a hand up to cover her own smile.

"Now watch," Serena said quietly to Natalie, "JJ will get up and leave. He can only take so much."

But he didn't leave. Instead, JJ lifted his chin into the air at an angle. He had sunglasses on, so Natalie couldn't see his eyes. "New girl," he said.

Natalie cringed and felt the blood rush to her face.

"Hey, you—"

"*Natalie.* Her name's Natalie!" Serena interjected sharply.

"Natalie," JJ repeated softly. "I'm sorry. Welcome."

"Thank you," Natalie said.

"You have a nice voice," JJ went on. "Do you have a boyfriend, Natalie?"

What? Was he looking at her as a candidate to be his girlfriend? How embarrassing! And what a personal question. Or was it? The truth was that Natalie had never had a boyfriend and JJ's question struck at a core fear of Natalie's. Because who would want to date someone who had trouble seeing?

"No," she finally said in a small voice. "I don't have a boy-friend."

Sheldon sat up. "She's too good for you, JJ," he said, elbowing the boy beside him. "You got to lower your sights, man."

"My sights? What are you talking about? You know I ain't got no sight."

Sheldon started laughing. And JJ laughed with him.

Were they kidding? Did JJ just make a joke about his blindness?

She turned to Serena for a clue, but the bored expression on Serena's face hadn't changed. "Don't pay no attention to him, JJ," she said. "He doesn't know what he's talking about."

JJ stopped laughing and stood abruptly. "I don't want to be late to class," he said.

But what about the ketchup? Wasn't somebody going to tell him about the spill down his shirt? Maybe no one wanted to embarrass him. Natalie watched, uncomfortably, as JJ snapped open his folding cane, picked up his backpack, and left.

The whole strange scene at breakfast made Natalie even more homesick for her own friends. She couldn't help but think of them because it was also the first day of classes back at Western Allegany High School. Meredith, Suzanne, and Coralee would be wearing their new jeans and the sandals that all four of them had bought on sale at Target. Natalie could almost feel their first-day excitement, the jokes, the confusion, the lockers slamming shut, the hustle and bustle in the hallways . . . the same hallways she and her mother had been in just a few days ago.

They had stopped at the high school one morning to pick up Natalie's transcript from the main office. It was the week before classes started, so the locker-lined halls were empty and spotless, the floors newly polished. As they passed the cafeteria, Natalie could hear faint radio music and the muffled clanging of pots in the back as the cooks prepared for another year of pizza, subs, and Tater Tots.

"Hey, Nat!" A boy's voice suddenly rang out, echoing in the empty hallway.

Natalie's mother touched her shoulder. "To your right," she said quietly.

"It's Jake," the boy said as he came toward them. "Jake Handelman."

Natalie smiled. She liked Jake, who apparently knew how helpful it was when people announced who they were. She must have mentioned this once, how much she appreciated that.

"Hey. So what are you doing here so early?" he asked.

Natalie could see him then. The baseball hat on backward, the cheeky face and wide smile, the bulky black T-shirt. It helped that Jake was so big—as big as the tuba he played in the marching band. At the end of their freshmen year, she and Jake had been elected class representatives to the student council.

"Couldn't wait to be back in school, huh?" he had teased.

Natalie's smile began to fade. She did not want to have to tell him that she was leaving.

But Jake didn't wait for an answer. "I was thinking," he said, "that we need to get those proposals written up for the first student council meeting."

Natalie felt herself sinking. They had both pushed for healthier food in the cafeteria as part of their campaigns. A lot of the kids wanted a daily salad bar and a machine that sold bottled water.

"We should get together one afternoon next week. Maybe Friday?"

"I can't," Natalie said. "I won't be here, Jake." She swallowed hard. "I have to go to a different school—"

When Natalie's voice faltered, her mother moved in. "Her

glaucoma, Jake. It's at the point where there is nothing more we can do."

"Wow. I didn't know. . . . Yeah. . . . But my grandfather had glaucoma. He had to take eyedrops like every day. I guess I didn't realize someone our age could get it, too."

Natalie was nodding. *Eyedrops.* He didn't have a clue! While memories of past surgeries flashed by, she sniffed and brushed the end of her nose with her hand, a nervous gesture. "Yeah, anyone can get it," she said weakly.

Jake hooked his thumbs in the pockets of his baggy shorts. His lowered voice sounded sincere. "I'm really sorry, Natalie."

"Thanks," she told him. "Good luck to you, Jake."

"And you, too," he replied as they turned to go.

"Stay in touch, okay?" he had called after them.

THE WORST

Unbelievable. On the second floor of Norland Hall at the Baltimore Center for the Blind, a whole walk-in closet full of canes hanging on hooks surrounded Natalie like a stalactite nightmare. Natalie heard the voice repeating: "Find one that fits." But her hands froze and the voice echoed in her head.

Definitely, absolutely, the worst thing so far, she thought. Forget the weird kids and a Braille lesson where she learned that there are six dots in a Braille cell and that different combinations of dots stood for different letters. A single dot, or bump, was *a* while *b, c, e, i,* and *k* all had two dots—but each set of dots was arranged differently! Impossible! How in the world were a bunch of bumps ever going to mean something?

But by far, the cane was her greatest fear because of all it represented—and all that it would strip away—like her freedom, and her anonymity. They may as well hang a sign around her neck, too: PATHETIC BLIND PERSON.

"Natalie, go ahead, hon," urged the woman who was Natalie's new cane instructor. "Lift a cane off the wall and see if it's the kind you want."

But Natalie didn't *want* a cane. She didn't *need* a cane. What would her friends think if they saw her right now? Would she even want to tell Meredith about this?

The instructor, Miss Audra, patiently repeated the instructions. "Just choose one," she urged. She was a young teacher. From what Natalie could see of Miss Audra, she was petite—probably no taller than Natalie herself—and Natalie had glimpsed a long braid down the instructor's back.

"Select one and let's see if it's the right length," Miss Audra prodded.

Natalie reached out, her fingers quivering, hesitating because she didn't want to touch a cane, let alone use it. Finally, she grabbed one, yanking it off the hook so fiercely that she knocked several other canes onto the floor with a loud clatter.

"Don't worry, we'll pick them up later," Miss Audra said, unfazed by the noise and the mess. "Focus on the cane in your hand, Natalie."

Natalie tapped the cane tip on the floor—a little too hard probably—and could tell it had a stationary pencil tip, as opposed to the canes that had a little wheel that rolled when the cane moved side to side.

"Is that the kind you want?" Miss Audra asked.

Want? I don't want a cane! Natalie screamed silently to herself.

"All right, then." Miss Audra's voice maintained its calm despite the lack of response from Natalie. "Let's see if it's the right size. Stand up tall, Natalie, shoulders back, and hold the cane in front of you. Closer. That's it. What did we just talk about? If it's up to your breastbone, up to your armpit, it's the right length. What do you think?"

The cane was slightly higher than her waist. Must be for a midget, Natalie thought a bit snidely. Or a small child, she realized.

"No," Miss Audra said when Natalie maintained her silence. "It's not the right one for you, is it? It's *way* too short."

Natalie fumbled around for another cane. By feeling bumps along its length she could tell it was the folding type, which most students had. The tip was straight, no roller, and it came up to her armpit.

"How about that one?" Miss Audra asked.

Natalie nodded, barely, but her heart was pounding and the blood throbbing in her temples. If she learned how to use that cane there would be no going back. She would be giving in. Admitting to the problem. Opening the door to loathsome blindness. Afraid, she squeezed her eyes shut, trying to block out how it would look, and what it would mean.

"All right, then. That's your cane. It has three parts: the grip, the stem—some people call it the shaft—and the tip. When we're finished today, take this cane back to your room. A lot of the kids put something on the handle, the grip, to identify it as theirs. A ribbon or some yarn, a key chain maybe."

Identify it as hers? Natalie almost laughed. No way!

"And *please*," Miss Audra emphasized, "keep the cane in a special place in your room, Natalie. *Always* in the same place so you know where it is. When you have O and M—Orientation and Mobility class—you need to bring it with you."

If she lost it, she'd be glad, Natalie thought.

"Now," Miss Audra continued, "a cane is really just an extension of your finger—a way of telling you what's coming up. Let's have you put the sleep shade on and get out into the hall and try it."

But when Miss Audra handed Natalie the spongy black mask, Natalie drew the line. She did not want to blind herself with the shade and take the cane into the hall and try it. She certainly did not want to take the cane back to her room and find a special place for it. Tears welled in Natalie's eyes and spilled down her cheeks.

"Natalie, what's wrong?" Miss Audra put an arm around Natalie's shoulders and guided her to a chair. "Here, sit down. *Please.* Talk to me."

Natalie sat and held the sleep shade in her lap.

"What is it, Natalie?"

"It's just that . . . I don't want a cane," she said finally. "I don't want to learn how to use it."

"Why not?"

"*Why not?!*" Natalie swung her head around and screwed up her face, repeating the question as though Miss Audra was crazy to ask it.

"Yes. Why not?"

"Because I'm not blind! Because I don't need a cane. Because I don't want to lose my freedom!"

"Lose your freedom?" Miss Audra didn't miss a beat.

"Yes!" Natalie insisted, frustrated that Miss Audra didn't seem to understand. "The minute I use that cane, people will look at me like *Whoa, she's disabled!*"

"But Natalie—"

"I don't *want* people looking at me like I'm weird! Like I'm a freak!" Natalie put a hand up to her mouth, surprised at herself for saying those things out loud. What a hypocrite! What was happening to her? Wasn't it Natalie who wanted the student council to convene a special panel of the handicapped students back at Western Allegany High School? So they could educate the other kids about their disabilities? She had worked hard to convince each one of those students—Peter Maxwell, who used a wheelchair; Claire McDermott, who was deaf; and Britney Tedesco, who had dyslexia— to take part. Each of them had finally agreed to sit at a table, as a panel, and pass a microphone, to answer questions and talk about their disabilities. Natalie had arranged the whole thing and here she was calling those great kids *freaks*. The shame of it quashed her anger. And in the silence that followed, Natalie dropped her head.

Miss Audra paused before continuing in her steady voice, "Surely you know what the report says about your eyesight, Natalie. In the event that you lose the rest of your vision, we want you to be ready. That is why you are here. So that you will have some skills when the day comes—"

"*If* the day comes," Natalie interrupted.

"Okay, *if* the day comes. So you aren't totally helpless." She paused again. "You don't want to be helpless, do you?"

No. Slowly, Natalie shook her head. She did not ever want to be helpless. She was already helpless enough.

Miss Audra touched one of Natalie's knees. "Then let us prepare you, Natalie. Let us give you the skills you will need *in case that day comes.*"

She sounded so earnest, so sincere that Natalie wanted to soften, but she couldn't.

"Who is your doctor, Natalie? Someone in Baltimore?"

"No," Natalie replied. "It's Dr. Rose, in Rockville."

"What did Dr. Rose tell you, Natalie?"

Natalie began chewing on her bottom lip. She didn't want to repeat, or even think about, what Dr. Rose had told her because that's when it really started. The big change inside. The panic. The *fear . . .*

Suddenly, the phone rang—a rude intrusion—and Miss Audra touched Natalie's knee again. "Would you excuse me for a minute, Natalie? I've been waiting for that call and I need to take it. I won't be a minute."

Natalie quickly nodded. Then, as soon as her instructor walked away, Natalie stood up and bolted from the room.

WHAT DR. ROSE SAID

She hoped no one was watching. Quickly, Natalie made her way down to the first floor of the building and out the door, where she grabbed the brass handrail and guided herself to the bottom step. Without time to move her head around and focus, everything was a blur, but Natalie remembered the picnic tables off to one side where the first-day reception had been held. She found an empty table, didn't hear or sense that anyone else was there, and sat down. Sucking in fresh air, she pressed her hands together between her knees and hoped she wouldn't get in trouble for taking off like that. But she did not want to even *think* about what Dr. Rose had said because he had let her down. Big time.

Although—and Natalie had to admit this—Dr. Rose had never actually *promised*. No. All those years, when the piercing light was finally out of her eyes and the tools put to one side, Dr. Rose had never actually promised that she would not go blind. Something more uplifting such as, "We'll hope for the best," or her favorite, *"We'll see,"* always concluded the examination.

But on August 19, three weeks ago, there it was. A diagnosis dropped in her lap one Tuesday morning like a hundred pounds of cement. Dead, foreboding, unwanted weight. There was no escaping it.

"I'm so sorry," Dr. Rose had said gently. "But there's nothing more anyone can do, Natalie. Absolutely nothing. I'm afraid you're going to lose your sight completely."

Natalie felt the air go out of the room. Her wide, disbelieving eyes searched frantically for his face. It wasn't easy, sitting so close to him. She had to pull her head back to widen her range of vision. But there he was—the shiny bald head, the thick forehead wrinkles, and the soft and serious gray eyes that, behind gold-rimmed glasses, never lied.

It was her mother who had spoken first, from a seat somewhere behind Natalie. "When?" she had asked. Her voice wavered in the heavy silence that had filled the room. "How much time?"

Dr. Rose removed and folded his glasses, then tucked them into a chest pocket of the white lab coat he wore. "To be honest, it could be several months. My best guess, however, is that Natalie will lose her sight within a few weeks. It could, quite literally, disappear overnight."

Natalie put a hand to her mouth.

"It's important—*crucial*," Dr. Rose emphasized, "that she get all the help she can right now. We've talked about this before but there's no question anymore, and no time to waste."

"The school for the blind?" Natalie's mother asked.

"Yes," Dr. Rose affirmed. "Immediately. I'd get her there for the start of the school year if I were you. It's only a couple weeks away, but we can certainly make some calls for you."

"I'm going to be a sophomore, though, I can't—" Natalie started to protest. And that's when the tears came. Suddenly, and without grace. Not sniffles, either, but huge, heaving sobs. Her mother rushed to put an arm around her shoulders, and Dr. Rose quickly handed her a tissue, which Natalie pressed to her eyes.

"You always said—that there was hope," Natalie sputtered.

Dr. Rose nodded as he plucked more tissues from the box. "I did," he agreed.

"You told me—you said things would be okay!" she accused.

"And they will, Natalie, they *will*." His big hands gathered and encapsulated Natalie's two limp fists until she had calmed herself. "But I never promised that you wouldn't lose your sight."

BLIND AS A BAT

M ost of you know me already. Yes, I know. Serena Benson, she
is back again. This is my second—and *final* year here—yay!"
Serena, sitting cross-legged on the living-room couch, raised her arms
in mock victory. She had volunteered to begin the introductions at
the dorm meeting and seemed to revel in telling the others a little
bit about herself.

"I like the color black and I like tight jeans," Serena continued,
pausing for laughter. "I also like to dance. I hate hypocrites, mean
people, stewed tomatoes, Monday mornings, and winter in general.
Oh, and I love to read. I am a *huge* Stephen King fan."

There were sixteen girls in the dorm, so it took a while to go
around the circle. Natalie found herself tuning in and out. She
wanted to know who the girls were, yes, sure she did, but she didn't
want them for friends. Not *real* friends that she could confide in
and laugh with. And she didn't want to be here period, so trying
to remember names was like planting a stake. With her right hand,
she fished around in her pocket, found the pink stone, and ran her
thumb across the letters: H—O—P—E.

Other girls, other names. Maya. Carlisa. Anna. It was difficult
for Natalie to see the girls' faces clearly, but she was able to notice
that a couple were African-American, and that one appeared Asian.

They came from all over the state, including some counties with funny names like Cecil and Wicomico. And it was obvious that some of the girls had disabilities other than blindness, but none were acknowledged.

"Maya. Just Maya, I guess. I'm new this year. I was born in South Korea, but I'm from Prince George's County . . ."

Natalie's mind drifted. Did her parents miss her? Were they worried? When her father closed up the barn for the night, would he have a dog biscuit tucked in his jacket pocket? Nuisance would be waiting for it, her enormous eyes peering between the wooden slats of her pen. . . .

"Natalie, it's your turn," the counselor said.

"Oh! Sorry!" Natalie let go of the stone and pulled her hand out of her pocket. "I'm Natalie O'Reilly. From Hawley—it's a small town in western Maryland. It's okay to call me Natty—or Nat if you want. I love to read, to listen to books on tape, and I'm interested in government and politics. I'm on the student council at my school back home."

When introductions were finished, the counselor suggested that the two halls might want to start thinking about what to call themselves.

"I've already thought about that!" Serena called out, waving her arm enthusiastically. "Yeah, I think if we have to be animals again, then B Hall should be the Blind Bats."

Chuckles and snorts all around. Natalie was astounded.

"That wasn't very kosher, Serena," a girl named Murph said. "I have pretty good vision. I'm not blind as a bat!"

"They're not blind! Bats aren't blind!" Eve burst out, stopping everyone. "It's a myth."

"Eewww. But they're like flying rodents," Murph said, screwing up her face. "They give me the creeps! And they carry that disease."

"But they don't all carry it!" Eve snapped back. "They're less likely to carry rabies than raccoons! It's a myth, that's all."

Serena said coolly, "Yeah, you know what a *myth* is, Murph. For example, it's a *myth* that you have pretty good vision."

"Girls, please!" the dorm counselor called out. "We will have *dignified names* for our halls. I'm thinking maybe The Explorers and The Voyagers. *Now.* Just a heads-up so everyone knows what we'll be doing together this year. We will be cooking and cleaning, doing our own laundry, and taking some field trips, too. Just so I have an idea, how many of you have been to the grocery store?"

The grocery store? Was she kidding? Natalie hesitated before raising her hand. She turned her head, her small circle of vision scanning the group. But it was clear: hers and Serena's were the only two hands up in the air.

When the meeting ended, Natalie got up to leave—she wanted out of there fast—but the counselor called her back.

"I have a new schedule for you, Natalie, and I also wanted you to know that a roommate is coming tomorrow. You should clear off the other bed and make space available in the bathroom for her things."

Natalie's heart dipped because there went her privacy.

With one hand on the wall to guide her, Natalie rushed back to her room and closed the door. Sitting on her bed, she simply took in a few breaths and let them out. A roommate. What else would they do to make her life more miserable?

Then she remembered the new schedule. She smoothed out the wrinkled paper on her lap. Even though it was printed in large font, the letters still weren't big, or dark, enough for her to read, so she reached over to pull her pocketbook up from the floor and rummaged in it for the handheld illuminator/magnifier she always carried. Clicking it on, she focused on the blocks one at a time to see that they had now scheduled Braille and Orientation and Mobility (the cane) every day instead of three times a week. And what was this? A weekly meeting with a social worker? What for?

Angry, Natalie balled up the schedule in her hands and threw it across the room, where it bounced off the wall and rolled under the absent roommate's bed.

She tried hard to stop herself from losing it. Write a poem, she thought. Sometimes she wrote little poems in her head.

> *A mistake,* she began. *But here I am*
> *Alone,*
> *in a Spartan cinder-block cell of a room*
> *Despicable white cane*
> *folded like a crumpled animal on the shag rug.*
> *Insulting sign taped on the wall over my pillow:*
> MAKES OWN BED
> *"Do they think I can't see?"*
> *I can see . . .*

Twenty-four hours. She had been here for a little more than one day and already it was too much. Her father's parting words came back to her: "You'll be okay, Natty. You've got way too much going for you. . . ."

That was it exactly, Natalie thought, sitting up and opening her hands as though to argue the point with an invisible stranger. She had so much going for her! She was a good student, a girl who laughed with her friends, who loved peanut M&M's and fuzzy socks and a Nubian goat . . . so why her?! Why would God do this to her?

Sometimes Natalie wished there was someone—or *something* to blame. But she was born without an iris, and that simple fact was the root cause of her juvenile glaucoma. Sporadic aniridia, they called it. Simple, irrevocable bad luck. The gene that was responsible for eye development didn't do what it was supposed to do.

"You'll have to accept it, Nat," her mother had whispered in the hallway when they left Dr. Rose's office that last time.

But did she have to accept it?

No! For years, Natalie had chosen to ignore the facts they gently *hammered* into her. She just refused to change her way of thinking. She could never say it out loud, but the conviction was deep. Natalie was certain that as long as she worked hard, prayed hard, and totally believed in herself it would never actually happen. Because how could it? How could a girl with so much going for her—simply lose her sight?

The fingers of Natalie's left hand gathered and squeezed the fingers of her right. She thought back to what people had told her: *The pressure is up again . . . this isn't good . . . surely you're struggling . . . the loss of peripheral vision is only the beginning . . . you've got to prepare yourself.*

But there was always hope. Wasn't there? It's why her father bought her the little pink stone. It's why she did her stupid eyedrops faithfully, twice a day. Even Dr. Rose once told her there was always hope. *Anything is possible,* he had admitted. *Miracles do happen . . .* So wasn't it possible that his own diagnosis was wrong? And no different from all the other times when naysayers had filled her ears with their dire predictions?

She was fourteen now, on the brink of so much, and maybe, from now on, she would have to get through it by doing what she had always done: tune out the naysayers, like turning off a radio station with too much static.

And hope for the miracle.

A PREVIEW OF WHAT'S COMING

In the morning, Natalie moved an empty box and made sure there was nothing else of hers on the roommate's bed or bureau top. In the bathroom, she shifted her two towels to one rack so that the other was free, and slid her toothbrush, toothpaste, and bottle of eyedrops all the way to one side of the narrow glass shelf above the sink. All halfhearted efforts. At another time, another place, Natalie might have loved the companionship of a roommate. But not then. Not when there was so much turmoil and uncertainty. Natalie dreaded having another human being foisted into her private space.

Quickly, she made up her bed, and then reached up to rip the humiliating sign off the wall above her pillow. MAKES OWN BED. It was pretty obvious, wasn't it? She tore it up and threw it in the trash.

Sighing, she jammed the books she needed that day into her backpack. When her foot stumbled over the cane, Natalie picked it up from the floor and heaved it into the back of her closet where it landed with a loud thud.

What if her new roommate talked all the time? Or snored at night? Or was so blind she walked into everything?

Natalie zipped up her purse. The schedule. Where was that new schedule? She rolled her eyes, recalling how she had thrown it across the room, then got on her hands and knees and felt around on the floor until she found it.

What if this new roommate was messy and left gooey toothpaste and stuff all over the sink? What if she used Natalie's towel by mistake? Or her hairbrush—*or her ChapStick?!* Natalie figured she'd have to start keeping those things in a drawer now.

She hoisted her backpack and started to walk out.

Yeah. And what if this new roommate was the type who borrowed things without asking? Or *stole*? Natalie's new iPod might be pretty tempting, and it was so small.

Natalie paused at the door with her hand on the knob. . . . She held the doorknob so long it made her hand cold. . . . What if her new roommate didn't want to be here either?

Slowly, she walked back to her bed, where she let the heavy backpack fall off her shoulders onto the mattress. Tearing a sheet of paper out of a notebook, she sat down and began writing in large letters with her black felt-tip pen: Welcome to 202. My name is Natalie. I'm new, too.

What else? Natalie bit her lip again. She hoped her roommate could see well enough to read the note. I'll see you later, she added, then stopped and blacked it all out. Phrases like that were always popping up. People didn't mean anything cruel by them, but those prickly everyday sayings could be as mood-altering as a vague stomachache.

She started over again with a new piece of paper, ending it with: Can't wait to meet you.

After placing the note on the empty bed, she joined the others in the lobby and took Serena's elbow for the long trek to the dining hall.

Let me not to the marriage of true minds
   Admit impediments. Love is not love . . .

In English, they were studying Shakespearean sonnets, and the teacher, a young woman named Miss Amelia, had written Sonnet 116 on the blackboard.

"There is a beat behind every poem, a cadence of words in a patterned sequence," she told the class. "Shakespeare used a lot of iambic pentameter. The *iamb* is the stress and the unstress, the *metric foot. Let ME not TO . . . Penta* means five—so five feet, five beats to the line."

While she spoke, three students pounded on their Braillers, which were like typewriters except that instead of keys they had six tabs that corresponded to the six dots in a Braille cell. Others tapped on Braille notebooks, which were like laptop computers except that they also had the six tabs corresponding to the six dots in a Braille cell. Serena and Natalie were the only two who actually wrote by hand. They took their notes with thick, black felt-tip pens on paper with wide, dark lines.

"Who wants to come up and mark in the stress and the unstress?" the teacher asked in a loud voice so she could be heard above the noisy Braillers. "How about you, Sheldon?"

Sheldon, who had just put his head down in his arms (a habit of his apparently), reluctantly pushed himself up and walked to the blackboard. He stood with his face about an inch from the words the teacher had written in chalk. Slowly, he moved his head in a circle. Natalie was fascinated. She knew that Sheldon had lost his central vision, so that he saw only peripherally, around the edges—the exact opposite of Natalie's problem. And she suddenly realized why he often seemed aloof, looking off into space, even when he was talking to you. He was just trying to see what was right in front of him.

In American government, the teacher's name was Mr. Joe (it was almost like kindergarten, Natalie thought, the way they addressed their teachers: Miss Amelia, Mr. Joe, Miss Audra, Miss Karen). Mr. Joe told class they would be studying the separation of powers in the three branches of government. "What are those three branches?"

Eve raised her hand to answer and for some reason stood up. Natalie, sitting behind her, noticed the huge red stain on the back of her white denim shorts. Her period?

Natalie felt embarrassed for her. She knew she would quietly say something to Eve at the end of class. But what if no one told her? How did blind people deal with this?

Sandpaper . . . silk . . . wool . . . With her fingertips, Natalie tried to feel each piece of material, slowly—*thoughtfully*, the way her Braille teacher instructed.

"It's all tactile," Miss Karen emphasized. "Your sense of touch becomes all-important with Braille. Try the workbook page again. Just recognizing when a line of Braille ends is a major accomplishment."

Miss Karen, herself blind, was enormously patient, but Natalie didn't think any of these crazy bumps on paper could ever translate themselves into letters and words, never mind complete sentences.

As always, the day ended with dreaded O and M lessons. Cane instruction.

"You need to coordinate your steps with the cane. When the

cane is at your left, you're stepping with your right. Remember," Miss Audra repeated, "the cane previews what is coming and where you are going."

What an awful phrase, Natalie thought. *Previews what is coming.* What *they* thought was coming was a horrible world of darkness. Natalie did not want to go there. She certainly didn't want a preview of the place!

Natalie swung the cane so hard it whacked into the wall on her right.

"No! Stop, Natalie! Again, now. More *gently*," Miss Audra begged. "Sweep only two inches wider than your body. Think about it. . . ."

No. She did not want to think about it.

Natalie's roommate arrived after school when the kids were gathered for Teen Group in the library. Teen Group was mandatory. It was supposed to be fun, an activity followed by dinner, although it appeared no one had been told about the fun part. The kids sat stiffly at tables arranged in a horseshoe, canes folded and placed under their chairs. As they did introductions, Natalie recognized most of the faces, although there were a couple new ones, too, including Thomas, who had brought his knitting.

"Do we *have* to come every week?" Murph asked sourly.

"Yes," said Miss Simon, a social worker in charge of the program. "It's part of your schedule, Murph." She sounded tired, but forced a little more enthusiasm when she introduced four young women from a nearby state college. Their names seemed to run together— Mindy-Ellen-Sasha-Latanya. "They're special education majors here to help us."

Suddenly, a door opened at the side of the library.

"People," Miss Simon said, "I want you to meet a new student. Her name is Gabriella. This is her first day."

Natalie was sure this was her roommate and sat up to get a better look. But the girl's head was down, her face obscured by long, wavy hair that was either white or very blond, Natalie couldn't quite tell. She appeared neither fat nor skinny, just kind of ordinary, with no other apparent disability, which was a relief to Natalie.

"Gabriella is from Baltimore," Miss Simon said. She turned to the girl. "Is there a nickname you would like us to use?"

Gabriella remained as still as a statue.

"Is there anything you'd like to be called other than Gabriella?"

But the adult might just as well have been talking to the wall.

"Gabby maybe?"

Nothing. The silence that followed made Natalie uncomfortable. Maybe there *was* something wrong with her.

"Well, I hope each of you will take the time to introduce yourselves to Gabriella later." Miss Simon pulled out a chair, whispered something, and Gabriella sat down.

"Okay, guys. I'm Mindy!" One of the college students took over by clapping her hands together, like a cheerleader, Natalie thought. "I thought tonight we'd share some pizza—it's on its way—and maybe just talk a little. Get to know each other. Like, maybe you guys can give us an understanding of your world."

Sheldon shot to an upright position and slapped both his hands on the table. "Our world is the same world as yours!" he exclaimed. "It pisses me off when people like you make comments like that."

Miss Simon stepped back. It was obvious she was going to let the college students handle it.

"Okay!" another of the college students piped up. "Thank you so much for your honesty. What else do you, uh, find frustrating? Tell us!"

Natalie looked around at the others, who had kind of slumped back in their seats. She knew no one else was going to say anything, and she actually started to feel sorry for the college students. After all, they wanted to be special ed teachers. Maybe they lacked some communication skills, but they did want to help kids with problems.

Natalie took a breath and raised her hand.

"Yes!" Mindy said eagerly. "I'm sorry, I forgot your name."

"Natalie."

"Natalie, yes. Please, go ahead, Natalie!"

"Well, I'll tell you one thing that frustrates me," she began, noticing the slight movement to her right as Sheldon lifted his head and turned toward her. "I have to wear a hat to keep bright light out of my eyes and it's awkward sometimes. People think I'm rude or have a hat fetish."

A couple of the kids laughed softly.

"It's also pretty embarrassing when I stumble over things," Natalie continued. "I've heard people say, 'Gosh, she's so clumsy,' and it hurts my feelings. I can't help stumbling over something I can't see."

"Yes, yes! I know exactly what Natalie is saying," Arnab added enthusiastically. "It is very frustrating when I walk into a wall!"

Some of the kids chuckled again.

"Also," Arnab went on, "it is so difficult when I do not know whether someone is talking to *me*."

"People need to identify themselves," said Paula from her seat in the wheelchair. "So we know who we're talking to, or who is talking to us."

"What really burns *me* up," JJ said, "are people who tap me on the shoulder and say, 'Guess who this is?' I mean, don't play those stupid games with me, man!"

"Yeah!" Murph agreed. She sat up and was rubbing her hands together excitedly. "I hate that! And I hate it when people ask me why I'm *smelling* that book. You know? Just because I have to hold it close?"

"People see you with a cane and they think you're weird—or else they treat you like a baby," Eve added.

"Or like you're mentally retarded!" JJ interjected. "You know, 'Here, sweetie, let me help you across the street.'"

"OH! I HATE THAT SWEETIE VOICE!" Murph shouted.

"Shhhhhhh!" Miss Simon warned her to keep her voice down.

Eve raised her hand timidly. "It really annoys me," she said softly, "when people talk so loud. They practically shout in my ear sometimes. Really, just because I'm blind, it doesn't mean that I'm deaf, too!"

"She's right," JJ agreed loudly. "What's wrong with people? I'll tell you what was really embarrassing for me. At this public school where I used to go? I walked into the girls' room!"

The kids burst out laughing.

"Yeah. Oh, man, you should've heard them scream," JJ went on. "But I said, 'Whoa! Don't worry! I can't *see* anything!'"

The kids laughed even harder. Even the college students joined in. When things started to settle down, Mark, one of only a couple kids who weren't laughing, spoke up from his wheelchair at the far end of the table.

"Public school. You want to talk about public school? Kids at my school would jump in front of me to see if I could see them," he told them. Natalie could tell by his voice that it was a bitter memory.

"They would snap their fingers in front of my eyes. One time they pushed me down a hill. Another time into the trophy case!"

The group fell quiet.

"Do you know why my arms are full of tattoos?" he asked them. "It's because I needed to show those kids that I was not a coward. Maybe I'm in a chair. And maybe I'm blind. But it doesn't mean I'm a sissy."

The room remained silent.

Mindy finally spoke up and tried to shift the conversation by focusing on Natalie's silent new roommate.

"Gabriella," she said, "what frustrates *you*?"

The girl lifted her chin and shook back her hair. She had a pretty face with clear skin. Her long hair was tucked behind one ear now, and Natalie thought she saw the sparkle of several earrings.

"I'll tell you what frustrates me," Gabriella said. "You. All of you. You're a bunch of freaks, if you ask me! I have no intention of staying here and being part of this . . . *group.*"

Her words hurt. Stung, actually. The table went silent again. Even Natalie felt the bite of her insults. She felt sorry for the group— for herself as well, because she was part of the group now, however much she wanted to deny it.

But Natalie would have to admit something else: she understood exactly how Gabriella felt.

MEANINGLESS BUMPS

S low down! You're going too fast!" Miss Karen warned. "You can't possibly decipher what you're feeling!"

Natalie reined in her galloping fingertips and moved them more gently, with exaggerated slowness across the meaningless bumps on paper. But even with intensive, one-on-one attention from Miss Karen, learning Braille seemed hopeless. Why even try? It certainly didn't help that Natalie was distracted by the recent cell phone call from Meredith: *Natty, here's the plan. We're all going to the county fair—you, me, Coralee, and Suzanne—Friday night. So call me as soon as you get off the bus on Friday, okay?*

Natalie didn't answer right away because as much as she wanted to be with Meredith and her friends, doing stuff at night was scary now. The glaucoma that had robbed Natalie of her peripheral vision bit by bit over the years had also destroyed the millions of tiny rods in her eyes. With those rods—those tiny photoreceptors—went the ability to see at night. She had confided this in Meredith recently, although she hadn't exactly told her how frightened she was going out at night. No one knew. But couldn't Meredith imagine? Didn't she care?

Natalie: *I'm not sure—*

Meredith: *But you have to! I can't eat all that funnel cake by myself. And you love the Ferris wheel! Besides, we're meeting some people there.*

Natalie: *People? Who?*

Meredith (giggling): *You'll see.*

Natalie (seriously, and very annoyed because Meredith wasn't remembering): *But I won't see!*

Meredith (sighing): *Sorry, Nat. You know I didn't mean that.*

Natalie: *Yeah. Then why did you say it?*

Pause.

Meredith: *Look, I have to go now. . . .*

And so Natalie had ruined the phone conversation. She was driving away her own best friend. She slumped and pulled her hands into her lap, so lost in thought she had forgotten she was sitting directly across from her Braille instructor.

Miss Karen sensed Natalie's frustration and must have figured it was the Braille. "Why don't we take a short break?"

As though on cue, Herky, Miss Karen's guide dog, noisily rearranged himself beneath the instructor's desk and stretched out his long legs. His metal dog tags jangled against the wood floor.

"You're fighting this, Natalie. Why?" Miss Karen asked.

Natalie felt her teeth clench. How could Miss Karen possibly understand how humiliating it was for Natalie to have to learn Braille? Like the cane, it wasn't even the difficulty of learning it so much as what it represented.

Miss Karen waited for a reply.

"I guess I don't understand why blind people have to learn Braille at all," Natalie said, sidestepping the issue. "I mean, there are books on tape and CDs, scanners that read print, and computer programs that talk. In English, a couple kids use a special laptop."

Miss Karen smiled. "Yes. Their *Braille* notebooks," she said. "Indeed, Natalie, there is so much new technology out there. But not everything is available in an audible version. And say you needed to label something—a box of cereal, for example—because how are you going to tell all those cereal boxes in the cupboard apart? Or the directions for a cake mix? Or a tag in your shirt telling you what color it is, or whether it's striped or solid. How will you know these things if you can't read and write Braille?"

None of that had occurred to Natalie.

"What if your technology breaks down or loses its battery charge? How are you going to take notes that you can read back?"

"I don't know," Natalie answered.

"If you lose your sight and you can't read Braille, Natalie, you will be considered illiterate."

Here we go again, Natalie thought, jumping to the worst possible conclusion. She plucked a water bottle from her backpack on the floor beside her.

There was an uncomfortable pause. Natalie took a sip of water and looked away.

"Is it because learning Braille would be admitting that you have a serious vision problem?" Miss Karen asked.

Natalie's eyes widened and she swung her head around. "Miss Karen, you don't understand how hard this has been."

"But that's where you're wrong, Natalie, because I *do* understand. I lost my sight when I was fifteen years old. Like you, I had to make the transition from reading print to recognizing Braille code. It was difficult—losing my sight, learning Braille, learning to use a cane. I won't kid you. Many times I wanted to give up."

Miss Karen was fifteen years old when she lost sight? A swarm of questions raced through Natalie's mind. How did it happen? What was it like? Was she devastated?

"Everything may seem overwhelming right now," Miss Karen went on. "You just have to take things one at a time. At least with the Braille, there is a system that you *can* learn, Natalie."

Miss Karen seemed so together—so upbeat—how did she ever get to that point?

There was another long pause. Miss Karen cleared her throat. "So. Are you envisioning the Braille cell?" She was going to continue the lesson. "The raised dots numbered one through six?"

"Yes," Natalie replied. She should at least try. "One through six."

"The first ten letters of the alphabet use only the top four of the six dots in the cell," Miss Karen noted. "The next ten letters, *K* through *T*, are identical to *A* through *J*, except that they have an additional dot in position three. . . ."

That night, while some of the kids went to the gym to play Bingo (with Braille cards), Natalie stayed behind in her room. Her roommate was sitting in the hall with her cell phone, talking to her boyfriend, so Natalie figured it was a good time to practice. The sooner she learned everything, she figured, the sooner she could return home for good. So she picked up the heavy gray Brailler that she'd been tripping over the last few days and set it on her desk. There was a short stack of heavy Braille paper in the desk drawer. She rolled a piece into the Brailler.

The Brailler worked like a typewriter, except that it had six tabs, one for each dot of the Braille cell, instead of letters. The tabs needed to create each letter had to be pressed simultaneously. After creating a letter, Natalie felt with her fingertips what had been punched out in the paper. She had to put some muscle into making each

Braille letter. It wasn't nearly as easy as using the sensitive computer keyboard. She did ten letters, messed up on five of them, and, arms resting on the desk, leaned her head on one hand.

Her heart just wasn't in it. The Brailler was difficult to use, and Natalie's right wrist hurt from the cane lesson that afternoon with Miss Audra. *Reach out and take hold of the cane as though shaking hands, Natalie. The movement should come from the wrist. Your hand may hurt. It takes a lot of practice.* But Natalie didn't want to "shake hands" with her cane. She didn't want to learn how to hold it, or sweep the area in front of her. She wanted to break the darn thing over her knee!

Natalie moved the Brailler to one side of her desk. Her mind drifted. *Learning Braille would be admitting that you have a serious vision problem. . . .* Meredith's chirpy voice echoed: *You'll see. . . .* Natalie's cranky reply haunted: *But I won't see!*

Natalie squeezed her eyes shut with deep regret. *A*, one dot . . . *B*, two down . . . *C*, two across . . . Those Braille cells—darn them!— they had staked out a spot in her brain and were doing calisthenics. Natalie couldn't get them out of her head now. Thank goodness there were only two more days until she could get on a bus and go home for the weekend. She wanted to sleep in her own bed, cook with her mother, get her hands on the goats, and tell Meredith so many things: how sorry she was about the phone call, how Eve had no concept of color and memorized her clothes by the way they felt, how much she hated the cane—and maybe—maybe she would confide in Meredith—about how much she had changed in the past three weeks, ever since the last visit with Dr. Rose. No one else knew how scared she was, underneath.

Would Meredith be able to help her? Would she even want to help her? Or would confiding her fear simply scare away her friends?

They could be fluky, especially Coralee and Suzanne. Probably best not to let any of them in on it, she concluded. They wouldn't be able to deal with it.

God knows those weren't the biggest questions either, because deep, deep down in her core, Natalie wondered if she would be able to deal with it, too.

SHADES OF BLUE

Finally. Natalie was going home for the weekend. She had all her books and clothes packed. Even the wretched cane was there, although it had been shoved deep inside her duffel bag under some dirty laundry. Miss Audra made Natalie promise to take the cane home, but Natalie certainly didn't plan on using it.

"Bus fifty-two!" Natalie's bus. Eager to go, she hoisted her backpack, grabbed her duffel, and moved quickly. But as she rushed to climb aboard, she missed the step completely and fell forward, scraping one leg on the step and landing in an awkward heap half on, half off the bus.

"Are you okay?" Several hands rushed in to help her up.

"I'm fine," Natalie said quickly, the blood rushing to her cheeks in embarrassment. "I didn't see the gap."

"You sure? Can you put weight on that foot?" someone asked.

Natalie stood. "Yes. Yes, I can, it's all right." She reached down and winced upon touching the shin, but could tell there wasn't an open cut.

She was grateful when one of the teachers helped her to get on board. After he left, she reached down to touch the spot again and felt a bump already forming. She wished she'd asked for some ice.

The others clambered on board after her. Most kids took up

an entire seat with their feet up and backs against the side of the bus. Right away, they popped in earphones to CD players or iPods and ripped open bags of snacks they'd grabbed from the vending machines—with Braille labels. Natalie plucked a water bottle from the side pocket of her backpack, took a swig, and pressed the icy bottle against her shin to dull the pain.

The first week was over, but it had felt like a year. The kids were different, for sure, and yet, when you took away their special needs, she thought, they were pretty much like everyone else. Miss Karen had told her that the blind school didn't used to have so many kids with multiple handicaps. When she was a student there, years ago, blindness was the only problem the students had. Now, she explained, many blind children are mainstreamed into public school with special help from vision teachers and don't need the blind center. So the center became a place for children with other needs, in addition to a vision problem. Plus kids like Natalie, Arnab, and Sheldon—the kids in the parallel universe—who suddenly needed intensive instruction.

About two hours into the trip, the bus pulled off the interstate.

"Why are we stopping?" Arnab asked no one in particular.

Serena turned around in her seat. "It's Frederick," she told him. "We pick up kids from the deaf school here."

Natalie could hear them climbing aboard, finding seats, talking among themselves in an odd way. When she finally got one in her circle of vision, she noticed the sign language—and could see Serena signing back to them. Suddenly, several of the deaf students burst out laughing. She wondered if they were laughing at something Serena had said—and if so, what it was!

"Arnab!" the bus driver called out. "I think this is where you get off!"

Serena tapped Arnab on the shoulder because he had his earphones in. "It's Frederick, Arnab. The bus driver just announced it."

"Yes, sir! Yes, I will be getting off in Frederick. Right here," he said. He seemed anxious as he scrambled to get all his things together.

"Have a nice weekend, Arnab," Natalie said.

"Natalie? Is that you? Yes, yes. I didn't know you were there. You have a nice weekend, too."

In Frederick, a huge traffic jam held up the bus, and another half hour crept by before they were back on the main highway. Outside, it grew dark. Natalie's ears popped as they went over a mountain. In a place called Hagerstown, Serena got off. "See you Sunday," she said to Natalie.

The "see you" part didn't bother Natalie. But the "Sunday" part did.

"Have a nice weekend," Natalie told her.

A few miles later, the bus broke down. The driver cussed and stomped off the bus heavily. Hours passed and it grew cold, sitting, waiting for another bus to come. Natalie pulled a sweatshirt on and tried calling home, but her cell phone battery had run out. So had the battery in her iPod. For sure, she wouldn't be home in time to go to the fair, and it filled Natalie with mixed feelings: she wouldn't have to deal with darkness, but she'd miss out on being with her friends.

A second bus finally brought Natalie to the small shopping center in Hawley. She was the last one off from a ride that had taken nearly seven hours. "Let's get you home," her mother said, after rushing forward to embrace Natalie in the dark parking lot.

———

Natalie's father waited in the kitchen at home with a sandwich. He hugged Natalie but was strangely quiet as she sat down to eat.

"Did Meredith call?" Natalie asked.

"No, I don't think so," her mother replied as she hurriedly prepared a bag of ice for Natalie's bruised shin. "Here, prop this leg up on the chair," she said. "That's it. And tell me about this roommate."

"You're sure Meredith didn't call?" Natalie asked again.

"I'm sure," her mother said. "Frank, did you take any calls?"

"No," he replied as he poured a glass of milk for Natalie. "None."

Natalie wondered why Meredith hadn't tried to get in touch.

"So—your roommate, Natalie. Who is she?" her mother persisted, kneeling on the floor and holding the bag of ice in place.

"Her name is Gabriella," Natalie said, still distracted. "All I know is that she is from Baltimore and that she's blind from a recent accident."

Her mother winced. "Car accident?"

"I don't know," Natalie said.

"Is she nice?"

"Hard to say," Natalie answered, finally turning her attention to the question at hand. "She doesn't talk to anyone. The first night we were alone in the room, she couldn't find the door to the bathroom and stood there, facing the wall, with her pajamas in her hand. I got up and guided her over, but did she say anything, like a simple 'thank you'? No."

"Well, I'm glad you reached out to her, Natty," her mother said.

Natalie finished the ham sandwich. "You okay, Dad?" she asked, wiping her mouth with a napkin. "Is something wrong? The goats?"

"Goats are all fine, Natty Bean," he said, using her childhood nickname. "I'm just thinking we cannot have this."

"Have what?"

"*This*—this coming home late at night. Broken down by the side of the highway. I'd rather have you here—"

"Don't start, Frank!" her mother cut him off. "It's the first week and the bus broke down. It's not like it happens all the time."

"Jean, I am not going to have Natalie sitting on the highway at all hours of the night!"

"Mom, Dad!" Natalie hated hearing her parents argue about her.

They both fell silent. It was pretty late by then. Natalie didn't have the energy to say any more. "I'm going to bed," she said. She left, cutting through the living room quickly, and easily avoiding the coffee table and the wing chair that jutted into her path. She knew the house like the back of her hand; she would never need a cane to find her way at home.

At night, Natalie kept her tinted eyeglasses in the same place: a shallow yarn basket by the sink in the upstairs bathroom. That way, in the mornings, she didn't have to search for them. She picked up the basket she'd made almost four years ago during a sixth-grade camping trip and brought it close to her face. She had chosen shades of blue, her favorite color: dark, deepwater blue, high-sky blue— azure they called it—and a pale robin's-egg blue. Sadly, she could barely tell those shades apart now.

Natalie set the basket down. It was eleven o'clock. The numbers on the digital clock to her left glowed bright red and were so large that Natalie could still read them. She wondered if her friends were still at the fair. Turning out the light, she put her glasses in the basket and did her eyedrops. It was twelve steps to the rug by her bed where she pulled back the covers and jumped in. She was home. She savored the smell and feel of her smooth cotton sheets and the soothing *ticktock* sound from the mantel clock downstairs.

But she could still feel the bump on her shin throbbing, and a Ferris wheel turned in her mind.

SECRETS

The clatter of a pickup truck woke Natalie early the next morning. It was a familiar sound coming through her open bedroom window along with the cool mountain air. Natalie knew it was her Uncle Jack arriving to help with the morning milking. The goats heard the truck, too, and, eager for breakfast and milking to be started, called out from their pens in the barn. That funny and frenetic *waaaahhhh* that Nubians made as they thrust their necks forward always made Natalie grin.

The good smell of coffee and of bacon drifted into Natalie's room as well. She lay in bed a bit longer, listening as the kitchen screen door slammed shut and her father and Uncle Jack greeted each other, their voices mixing, fading away as they walked across the yard toward the barn. No doubt, Natalie's mother had already left in the family van with coolers full of cheese for the farmers' market in Morgantown, West Virginia, just over the border, half an hour's drive away. Natalie had been given the morning to sleep in, but she often went to the weekend markets, helping to bag cheese for customers and slipping in a brochure about Mountainside Farm.

Soon, she would go downstairs for something to eat, then straightaway to the barn to see Nuisance. But first, there was the test.

All along there had been a secret test. Natalie did the test once a week, and always when no one else was around. She wasn't sure why it had to be done so secretly. It was just the way it had evolved over the years.

In the bathroom, Natalie quickly did her eyedrops, then found her tinted glasses and put them on. She stood for a moment, using her small circle of vision to check out her reflection in the mirror: the shoulder-length hair mussed by sleep, the wispy bangs, the face with a light sprinkling of freckles she knew were there but could no longer see.

Finally, she turned and walked over to the small bathroom window to her left. The window was framed by cheerful yellow-and-white-checked curtains. From there, Natalie had always been able to see the lawn bordered by her mother's flower garden, the maple tree, and the neighbors' back fence. The Stanleys were a nice family with three boys and a collie named Curlie. They had a small deck on the back of their house and a bright red back door. Odd, that a back door was red like that, but that's what made it so great, because it was easy to see. It was her peripheral vision that was disappearing, not the ability to see long-distance, but Natalie somehow figured as long as she could see over the fence to that red back door she was doing okay.

Natalie parted the yellow curtains and looked out. For months, it had been impossible for her to actually *see* anybody in the Stanleys' backyard when she heard voices, or the occasional basketball hitting the rim. About a year ago, she had lost sight of the dog, even though she could still hear it barking. But now Natalie could not even see the fence that separated the yards. Nor could she see the red door.

Had they had painted it?

Not likely, Natalie thought, realizing that the house itself had become a vague, dark block framed with an eerie gray haze.

Suddenly, a harsh cry pierced the air. Natalie put a hand to her heart and let the curtains fall back. When the sound repeated, there was no question: it was Winston, their "guard dog" llama, issuing his shrill warning. Natalie rushed downstairs. Winston's call meant that something threatened the pasture.

"Natalie, stay inside!" her father called out as he burst through the back door and rushed past her.

"What is it, Dad? A coyote?"

"Don't know!" he called back breathlessly.

Natalie stayed out of the way. "A bear?"

Her father didn't answer. But maybe he didn't hear in his rush to the gun safe. Natalie knew every move her father was making in the office. He was finding the key, hidden in an old library book about goat farming, far right, bottom shelf, behind his desk. After unlocking the safe, he'd see the guns arranged with the rifles to the left—the .270 caliber deer rifle next to the .22, which her father used for varmints like groundhogs. To the right were the 12- and 20-gauge shotguns. Bullets and shells were in packages neatly stacked on a shelf above them. Natalie had learned years ago how to load and fire each of those guns.

As he came back through the room, her father carried two weapons. Natalie didn't need to ask why. If he thought he could get a good aim, he'd use the rifle. If not, he'd fire the shotgun.

"Get down, Nat!" he told her before he rushed back out the door.

Natalie sank to the floor, hugging her knees. She heard and felt her father's feet pound across the yard. Winston called out again, and the goats bleated excitedly from inside the barn.

A few minutes later, a gunshot echoed. A second shot followed. Natalie waited on the kitchen floor until her father returned.

"Nothing but a coyote prowling around," her father said, not sounding too concerned. "I think I scared him off. But it reminds me. Nat, I want to show you something out in the barn."

Natalie stood and slid her hands down the kitchen counter, looking for her baseball cap, which she put on while her father locked up the guns.

"Coyotes are gettin' to be a problem around here," her father said, coming back through the kitchen. Natalie heard the screen door open and assumed he was holding the door open for her even though she couldn't quite get it in her circle of vision.

"Come on, let's go," he urged. Natalie moved quickly toward his voice. Down the steps and out in the yard, however, she hesitated, not knowing what lay ahead. A wheelbarrow, a bucket, a rake, any number of things could be in the yard. Her father touched her elbow to guide her, but then walked so fast Natalie practically had to jog to keep up. It wasn't exactly "sighted guide," and Natalie was nervous not knowing what was directly in front of her. Her father didn't seem to notice her anxiety.

"I've had black bears sniffin' around the past month, too," he complained. "What I'm thinkin' is that I want to keep a shotgun tucked away in the barn somewhere. Takes too much time running back to the house."

Her father guided Natalie through the barn until they stood by the grain bin. Natalie felt the edge of the cold iron container and could smell the molasses-soaked feed.

"Look," he said. "I'm going to put a shotgun up here."

He let go of her elbow and Natalie heard him pushing things around. Metallic cans clinked and glass bottles rattled. "Right here."

"You'd better describe it, Dad," Natalie said, "because I can't see what you're doing."

There was a pause. Natalie heard her father sigh. He just was not able to accept the fact that she couldn't see so well anymore.

"The long cupboard—up over the grain bin, Natty." He sounded impatient and it hurt. "You know, where I keep the salve and the medication?"

"Right, right. Okay." Natalie nodded vigorously. "I know it."

"I'll put the shotgun up here and stack some extra shells beside it. The safety will be on. I'll show Uncle Jack, and your mother, and *you* where it is. But you don't mention it to anyone else, you hear?"

"Yes. I promise," Natalie replied, amazed—*astounded*—that her father would include her in this knowledge, and loving him all the more for it. But how could she possibly find, load, and fire a gun at this point?

She felt her father's arm around her shoulder. He gave it a squeeze. "Just in case," he said softly. "I hope you never have to use it."

A FLOATING HEART

T omorrow. She has to catch the bus back right after lunch," Natalie's mother said into the cordless phone tucked between her ear and shoulder as she took clean coffee mugs from the dishwasher and stacked them one at a time in the cabinet above the counter. "When Natalie saw Dr. Rose last month, her IOP was twenty-four—*twenty-four*, can you believe it? It's never been that high. . . ."

It struck Natalie then, listening to her mother in the next room, how they had learned a whole different language over the years and foisted it on their friends and relatives. Like CD ratio and IOP. Most people wouldn't have a clue what those initials meant—and probably couldn't care less. But Natalie's sight depended on them. She could still remember how Dr. Rose had tried to explain it to her years ago.

"Everyone's eyes are filled with fluid," Dr. Rose had told her, doing his best to simplify things so Natalie, who was eight, could understand. "Fluid constantly enters the eye and then leaves through a tiny drain. The balance of that fluid inside the eye is called the *intraocular pressure*—the IOP. Now, if there is a problem in this natural drainage system, then the fluid builds up, creating pressure—think of a water balloon expanding—and, with nowhere else to go, presses against the retina."

He paused. "Do you remember what the retina is, Natalie?"

Natalie knew the retina was like a little movie screen in the back of the eye, but she still looked puzzled, so Dr. Rose pulled out a marshmallow from a little zipped Baggie in his top drawer. "Imagine the surface of the marshmallow is the back of your eye, Natalie." He pressed his index finger into the marshmallow. "That's what the cupped area of your retina would look like, where the optic nerve gathers and sends its all-important messages to the brain. If fluid in the eye builds up, it can press against this cupped area and make it wider and deeper." Dr. Rose then took his thumb and pressed a larger indentation into the marshmallow. "The bigger that indentation, the more likely there is vision loss."

An eye. A marshmallow. It was finally beginning to make sense. Years ago, Natalie had even tried to explain it to Meredith while they strolled around the playground at recess kicking stones. They were only in third grade, but Meredith said she really wanted to understand why Natalie was going to miss a whole week of school. "I'm serious, how come?"

So Natalie tried to explain about the upcoming operation that would give her eye a new drain. "They need to relieve the pressure, see, so they're going to make a little slot in my eye—"

"They're going to *cut* your eye?" Meredith's own eyes grew large. "With a *knife*?"

"Well, yeah, they have to. But it's not the kind of knife—"

"Eeeewwwwwww!" Meredith put her hands over her face.

And Natalie took off running. Meredith chased her and, when she finally caught up, grabbed the sleeve of Natalie's sweater. "I'm sorry," she apologized. But they never talked about Natalie's surgeries again. Just as well, Natalie figured, because it was pretty complicated. Back then, Natalie realized, it was a lot easier *not* knowing everything.

———

Suddenly, the doorbell rang.

"I'll get it, Mom!" Natalie called out. She'd been cleaning out her purse on the dining-room table, using her lighted magnifier to read and separate receipts. Scooping up the pile of trash, she chucked it into a wastebasket and whisked through the living room to answer the door.

She was surprised—and happy—to find Meredith standing on the front step in shorts and a tank top, her blond hair twisted up on her head.

"Hey!" Natalie greeted her.

Meredith held a tin and, perched on the tin, a brown teddy bear wearing a white turtleneck sweater embroidered with the words (Natalie had to hold it close to see): HUGS FOR FREE. "For you, Nat," she said.

"Wow," Natalie said. She gave the bear a welcome squeeze. "He's so soft!" Then she noticed something red tied to Meredith's wrist and followed it upward to a heart-shaped balloon that floated over her friend's head.

"I didn't really get a chance to say good-bye last week," Meredith said. "Remember? We were at that soccer scrimmage? And hey! We really missed you last night. I tried to get you, Nat, but no answer."

Natalie hoped that was true. "Yeah," she said. "The bus broke down."

"Yikes. . . . Well, anyway, look, Coralee and Suzanne were going to come, too, but they forgot they had their first driver's ed class."

The news caught Natalie off guard. "Driver's ed?"

"Yeah, I don't know what the big rush is, but they are dying to drive."

They had never mentioned it, Natalie thought. Were they being sensitive because they knew Natalie would never get a license? Or was she out of the loop already?

A slight pause. "Do you want to come in?" Natalie asked.

"Only for a minute," Meredith said. She let Natalie close the door, then scrunched up her nose and indicated with her thumb how her dad was waiting outside in the car. "We have to go to my grandmother's for dinner."

The two girls walked into the living room and Meredith touched Natalie's arm. "So, guess who was asking about you this week?"

"*Me*? Someone was asking about *me*?"

"Yeah, *you*! Jake Handelman! He asked if I'd heard from you."

"He's such a nice boy, isn't he?" Natalie replied.

"*Really* nice—and cute, too. If only he'd lose about fifty pounds!"

Natalie grinned.

The two girls sat side by side on the sofa. Natalie took the bear and held it in her lap. The helium-filled balloon was still tied to Meredith's wrist and undulated in the air, moving with her hand as she leaned forward to put the tin on the coffee table.

"You're really sweet, Meres," Natalie said. "But it's not like I'm going away forever." It was really bothering her, the good-bye stuff, the separation from her friends. She didn't want to think of it as permanent. "I'll be back every weekend."

"I know," Meredith said. "But it's still not the same . . . 'cause you're not in school with us."

Natalie nodded. She couldn't deny it was the beginning of a major change for both of them. They had been best friends for a long time, ever since second grade when Meredith moved to Hawley from West Virginia. Meredith had crooked teeth then, and on her first day of school, some boys blew spitballs at her through a straw and called her a hillbilly when she entered the cafeteria. Natalie told her they didn't mean anything and offered Meredith a place to sit at the lunch table.

"I'd better go," Meredith said. "I know you leave early tomorrow—"

"But maybe we can get together next weekend," Natalie suggested.

"For sure!" Meredith agreed.

The girls walked back to the front door together, and Meredith turned and paused. Her eyes glistened and her lower lip quivered. "I'm going to miss you, Natty."

Natalie blinked and tears suddenly bathed her eyes, too. She opened her arms to give Meredith a hug, and the two girls embraced. "I'm going to miss seeing you, too," she said.

It wasn't intentional, but Natalie realized the moment she said it that the words were heavy with meaning.

"WHATEVER IT TAKES"

R ape is not sex! Rape is an act of violence! A rapist needs to control and *humiliate* his victim." The karate instructor's loud voice echoed with authority in the small, old-fashioned gym at the Center for the Blind.

"It might make you uncomfortable to hear some things I talk about," Mr. Lee continued. "But my job is to teach you the skills you need to protect yourself! The number one skill?" He held up his index finger. "Information!"

Natalie fixed her small circle of vision on the short, but lanky, ponytailed man. He stood with his hands on his narrow hips, while the girls in Natalie's gym class sat before him in rapt attention, cross-legged on the polished wooden floor. They wore T-shirts, shorts, and sneakers and had just completed twenty minutes of exercises—stretches, sit-ups, modified push-ups, jumping jacks—before Mr. Lee sat them down to talk. Their skin glistened with sweat and the smell of perspiration hung in the air.

"This is the book we will use in class—*Safe Without Sight*." Mr. Lee held up a copy and thumped a finger on its title. "Each of you will get a copy. I have it in Braille, large-print books, and tapes.

"You will read—or listen to—every word in this book. You will learn how to protect yourself through nonviolent ways first.

That means using your brain! We'll discuss three important skills: awareness, intuition, and how to set boundaries.

"But you're also going to learn the tough stuff. How to use your hands, feet, canes, fingers—*whatever it takes*—to save your life."

Whoa. This was really going to be an interesting class, Natalie was thinking. To her left, she could hear Eve still quietly taking in gulps of air to recover from the exercise. To her right, Serena wiped sweat off her face with the bottom of her T-shirt.

Mr. Lee lowered his voice a notch. "I'm not going to pussyfoot around in here. If you don't want to take this on, go ahead and leave. No hard feelings. But if you stay, you are part of this class. We will work hard. And we will work together!"

Suddenly, Murph pushed herself up and stood, her two sneakers slapping the wood floor. "I'm leaving then," she announced. "My mother would throw a fit if she heard you talking about these things."

Natalie quickly focused back on Mr. Lee to catch his reaction. He seemed surprised. "Okay!" he replied crisply. "But you talk to your mother, young lady, and ask her: Does she want you to have knowledge? To be prepared? Or does she want you to be an ignorant victim on the street?"

Murph faced away from the teacher, which seemed strange, and she paused, as though expecting the others to stand up, too. But no one else made a move. Finally, Murph began walking out of the gym. Her cane, tapping on the floor and growing fainter as she moved farther away, was the only sound as everyone absorbed her departure. For some reason—Natalie couldn't quite pin it down—she felt sorry for Murph.

"True or false?" Mr. Lee called out sharply, steering the girls' attention back to the lesson. "Nice-looking people are more likely to be raped."

Serena's hand shot up. "True!" she called out.

"False!" Mr. Lee fired back. "The book says ninety percent of rapists think about their attack first. It has nothing to do with sexy, nice-looking people. Rapists are looking for an easy target. They are looking for a woman who appears weak. So! You're blind. Does that make you an easy target?"

No one attempted to reply this time.

"Ah. Mr. Lee is thinking you girls say, 'Yes. Blind people are an easy target.' If you think this way, you probably are!" He threw open his hands and raised his voice. "But you don't have to be an easy target!

"Walk with a sense of confidence and purpose!" he told them. Natalie was able to see his ponytail swing as he turned around and strode across the gym floor in front of the girls. His chest and chin were up, and one arm moved side to side in front of him as though maneuvering an invisible cane.

He stopped and faced them again. "Blind people can't drive cars. They must use public transportation. Subways, buses, taxis—all these things put you at more risk. But there are many things you can do to protect yourself. It's easy! We will start learning tonight!"

He clapped his hands a single time. "Now. Once a criminal decides to commit a violent crime, he needs two things. He needs a victim and he needs an opportunity." Mr. Lee tapped his head. "So! Use your brain first!"

He picked up the book and read from it. "Listen to the sounds around you. Footsteps, voices, vehicles, water draining in the gutter, windows opening and closing. Pay attention to your relative proximity to the sources of these sounds and how it changes, getting closer or farther away. As you pass other people who may be talking, notice their tone of voice and what they are saying.

"Your sense of smell can give you important information, too," he continued. "Things like *cologne*. Ah, he smells nice!"

The girls giggled.

"But what about those other smells: cigarette smoke, mothballs on clothing, alcohol on the breath, personal body odor—"

When the girls laughed at the body odor reference, Mr. Lee shook his head and waggled his finger at them. "No, no, no!"

The girls stopped laughing.

"An important clue!" Mr. Lee emphasized.

And *then* he began talking about a special skill some blind people could develop called acute spatial awareness. "Some blind people can *feel* the presence of a tall building, a tree, or another person."

Natalie was fascinated—but skeptical. Because how could anyone *feel* the presence of a building?

"Eve is good at it," one of the girls offered. Natalie didn't catch who had spoken.

"Eve? Would you like to tell us more about it?" Mr. Lee asked.

There was a pause, and Natalie wondered if Eve would even reply because she was so shy.

"Well, it's not just a thing that's there," she began quietly. "But also when it's *not* there, like a space."

"Can you explain that?" Mr. Lee asked.

"I'll try. I'm not sure. But I can *feel* an open space," Eve said. "Like in a building? I can tell when I get to a place where the halls meet, where the hall gets bigger. I can tell where there's a doorway. Sometimes even a window."

"But how?" Natalie asked from her seat on the floor beside Eve.

"It's kind of like a difference in the air," Eve said. "You can feel it. That and the sound of your footsteps and the tapping of your cane—the sound is louder if you're in an enclosed space because the sound is bouncing back to you. It's like echolocation, what the bats use."

"Mr. Lee, I did the same program as Eve," Serena suddenly piped up. "It was at the National Federation of the Blind place downtown. They taught us that stuff about echolocation, but I didn't hear anything different."

"Because you never tried!" Eve accused.

"Bunch of patooty," Serena retorted.

"You needed to have confidence in it for it to work," Eve countered. "You needed to use the straight cane all the time—and you needed to wear the sleep shades, which you refused. Remember?"

"Yeah. So if that program did so much for you, Eve, then why are you here?" Serena shot back. "Why aren't you in public school? Down in Caesar Salad, Maryland, or wherever—"

"Waldorf," Eve murmured.

"Waldorf! Waldorf salad! That's it!" Serena chortled.

"Stop!" Mr. Lee clapped his hands. "We won't have that here!"

The room fell silent again. Natalie wished Serena hadn't interrupted. She was really insensitive sometimes.

"Enough for today," Mr. Lee said. "I'll see you girls next week!"

Natalie stood with the others to leave. Interesting class, she thought, although she sure didn't want to think she'd ever need what Mr. Lee was teaching them.

"Don't forget to pick up a copy of the book!" Mr. Lee was calling after them. "What you learn here may save your life one day!"

EVERYWHERE

Renegade *W* is what Miss Karen called it. Unlike all the other letters of the alphabet, *W* didn't follow the pattern in Braille. She explained: "*W* is out of order because Braille was originally written in French in the early 1800s, which at that time did not contain a letter for *W*. So we had to invent one!"

Okay. So sometimes it *was* interesting, and Natalie *was* beginning to appreciate how Braille could actually open a whole world to people who couldn't see. Still, what Natalie thought about most at her new school was *not* Braille, or a cane, but Home and her Friends and how Forward Motion would keep her from acknowledging the constant butterflies in her stomach. She couldn't wait for Friday to come, and every day looked forward to the phone calls she could make after 8 P.M. One afternoon, she even found herself rehearsing in her head the conversation she'd have with Meredith.

I wanted to tell you about this boy at my new school. He's Indian—meaning he's from India—and on the bus back to school he brought me this dessert his mother made. It was in a cute little box, too, just for me. Coconut and poppy seeds and something called jaggery, which he said is like concentrated sugarcane juice . . . and oh, it's so funny, but this girl, Eve, across the hall from me—I thought she had a bird in her room, but it's her clock! An Audubon clock. She tells time by the kind of bird that sings—like the bluebird sings at eight . . .

She would keep the conversation upbeat, she had decided. She didn't want to make it hard for Meredith to be a friend.

Back in her room, Natalie heard Gabriella taking a shower and figured it was a good time to start homework so she would have more time for phone calls. Which is when it hit her: she had forgotten her backpack on the second floor of Norland Hall after her O and M lessons. It was because she and Miss Audra had ended their walk in the dining hall at dinner. Natalie had planned to retrieve the backpack after she ate, but forgot.

The evening counselor insisted Natalie take someone with her back to Norland Hall, so Natalie asked Serena.

"I'm sure I would be okay by myself," she told Serena as she took the girl's elbow and they walked together back down the sidewalk.

"Yeah, I know. But stupid rules, right?"

"Look, you don't have to go all the way upstairs," Natalie offered. "I'll just run up, grab it, and come back down."

"But you don't have your cane," Serena said. "Will you—"

"I don't *need* the cane," Natalie stopped her. "I'm okay once I'm inside and there's some light."

"Okay," Serena said. "I'll wait here on the bottom step."

Natalie moved quickly up the wide staircase to the second floor, then down the hallway, keeping a hand on the wall. The O and M office was at the far end. The door was open and Natalie glimpsed her bright red backpack. She grabbed it and, with one hand trailing the wall to her left this time, retraced her steps quickly back through the hall. When the wall ended, she began crossing a wide, tiled foyer and wondered, if she had her cane, would she be able to sense the open space like Eve? She'd try another time, just for the heck of it. Meanwhile, she moved swiftly, not wanting to keep Serena waiting, and reached for the wooden handrail that she knew was to her left.

In her haste, however, Natalie misjudged the location of the top stair and missed the first step completely, which sent her spiraling over the edge. She landed hard, her left shoulder smashing into the stairs, her head against the wall. There wasn't even time to scream. Natalie's glasses and hat flew off and her backpack bounced down the stairs. A horrible thud and all was silent.

Things were always a blur to Natalie, but this time nothing made sense as she slowly opened her eyes. Parts of different faces hovered over her and strange voices wove together in a surreal way. Pain shot through her left shoulder and arm. She winced as someone lifted her. Without her tinted glasses the lights hurt, forcing her to squint and shield her eyes with one hand. She had never been in an ambulance before but was aware that she was in one.

After a short ride to the hospital, the stretcher was rolled into an emergency room, where the lights were even brighter. "*Please*—my eyes," she begged, grimacing and holding her hand over her face. Someone kindly draped a towel over her eyes.

Then Natalie heard a familiar voice.

"Miss Audra, is that you?" she asked.

"Yes, Natalie. I'm here." She sounded breathless. Natalie reached out a hand and Miss Audra took it. "They called me and said you fell. I came right away! I practically followed the ambulance. Are you okay?"

"I think so. But my arm hurts."

"What happened, Natalie?"

"I don't know. I was getting something—wasn't I? My backpack. I had my backpack and I fell down the stairs. Serena was with me."

"Apparently, it was a bad fall, Natalie. You lost consciousness for a few minutes."

"I did?"

"Gosh, Natalie, did you have your cane with you? Were you using it?"

Natalie didn't answer right away. The only time she ever used her cane was during O and M lessons, after which she tossed the cane into the back of her closet.

"I didn't have it," Natalie confessed.

Silence as Natalie envisioned Miss Audra frowning and crossing her arms.

"That ends tomorrow," Miss Audra declared. "From now on, Natalie, the cane goes with you *all* the time and is used *everywhere*."

Natalie felt her heart dip. She did not want to use that cane. But neither did she want another bad accident. Deep down, she knew that the accident marked a turning point. No way could she keep on living the way she had, pretending she didn't need any help but knowing that she did.

Miss Audra stayed with Natalie for the next several hours while X-rays were taken and nurses watched for signs of head injury. An ice pack was brought in for her left shoulder, another for her wrist. The ice made her cold. Miss Audra left to find a blanket and even managed to locate a cup of warm tea somewhere.

Finally, a doctor came in to announce that no bones were broken.

"Although you do have a shoulder sprain," he said. "And there was a slight concussion. You need to take it easy for a couple days."

It was nearly midnight when they arrived back at school. The evening counselor handed Natalie her hat and her glasses, which, amazingly enough, were still intact.

"Is there anything else I can do?" Miss Audra asked.

"I'll be fine," Natalie assured her, whispering at the doorway to her room so as not to wake Gabriella. "Thank you so much for everything."

Miss Audra gave her a gentle hug. "See you tomorrow."

But Natalie was sorry she hadn't asked for more help, because it was next to impossible to get her T-shirt off over the sling. She gave in and decided to just sleep in her clothes. In bed, she managed to maneuver an extra pillow under her arm, then cradled the teddy bear in the crook of her neck and used it to help hold an ice pack against her throbbing temple. When she was finally in the most comfortable position she could manage, she realized she'd left a bottle of water on the bureau.

"Oh, no," she groaned, "my drink." She sighed, wondering if it was worth the effort to maneuver herself out of bed.

"Can I get it for you?" a small voice in the darkness asked.

Natalie rolled her head toward her roommate. "That would be great," she murmured softly. "My water bottle—it's up on our bureau."

Gabriella folded back her covers and crossed the room. Natalie could hear her bare feet pad across the tile floor, then her hands as they explored the bureau top and knocked something over— probably her own cologne bottle.

"Got it," Gabriella said.

She brought it to Natalie and, while making sure it was in her grasp, their fingers touched.

"Thanks very much, Gabriella," Natalie said. "I really appreciate it."

"We heard about your accident," she said. "Are you hurt bad?"

"My shoulder mostly. I think I'll be okay," Natalie said.

Gabriella didn't say anything else but returned to her bed. Natalie listened as the girl pulled her covers back up.

Silence again, until Gabriella said, "You can call me Bree."

⠿

CLUES AND LANDMARKS

In the morning, Natalie rubbed her sore shoulder, then gingerly crouched, and with one hand searched her closet floor for the cane she had heaved in there.

"I'll be in the lobby," Bree said, "unless you need help."

Natalie looked up. "Thanks," she responded, still amazed at the overnight change in her roommate. Her fall down the stairs must have jarred loose a chunk of sympathy, Natalie thought.

But there was a change in Natalie, too. She felt it as she found and retrieved her cane, then stood, unfolding each section a little more carefully than she had in the past.

At breakfast, everyone made a big fuss over Natalie's accident and peppered her with questions and offers of help.

"Shall I dish out the scrambled eggs for you?" Sheldon offered.

JJ's voice: "Were you scared?"

"Do you want your toast buttered?" asked Eve, her face smack in front of Natalie's.

Natalie repeated her story several times, including how difficult it was to get comfortable in bed. "I was so grateful when Gabriella brought my water bottle over."

The table fell quiet. Natalie was sure that no one had forgiven her roommate for the insulting remarks she had made on her first day at school. But Natalie was eager for them to know there had been a softening in the girl's hard-core attitude.

"I want to talk about clues and landmarks," Miss Audra announced at the beginning of cane instruction that afternoon. She said they would "give the wrist a rest" and take a walk outside using sighted guide. It was a warm September day and the sun felt good after being inside so many air-conditioned classrooms.

"Now, a *clue* is something that may or may not be there to help you find your way, whereas a *landmark* never moves," Miss Audra explained. She reached out to rattle the metal trash basket near them on the sidewalk. "This trash basket is a clue. The car parked on the circle here"—she thumped on the vehicle's roof—"it's a clue, too, because the car might not be here next time, just like the trash basket."

They moved on. "The big bush here in front of Norland Hall is a landmark," Miss Audra said as she took Natalie's right hand and had her touch the thick green boxwood. "The elevator, the water fountain, they're landmarks. You can pretty much count on them being there. You need to remember these landmarks—they're part of the 'orientation' portion of 'orientation and mobility.' Making a map with landmarks in your head.

"Let's rest a minute," Miss Audra said, gently guiding Natalie to a bench outside the gym.

Natalie had been waiting for a chance to say something. "Miss Audra," she began, "first, I want to thank you for being there for me last night. And second, I want to apologize for being such a pain-in-the-you-know-what last week."

Miss Audra scoffed. "No more than anyone else."

"I know for a fact that I've had a bad attitude. I guess I'm a little angry at what's happening. And I'm frustrated with a lot of the things I have to learn."

"What else besides the cane? The Braille?"

"Definitely the Braille—although I do understand the need for it. I was thinking about other things, like that social worker I have to see."

"Ms. Kravitz?"

Natalie nodded. "I know that some of the kids here might need someone like that, but I don't. It's insulting for someone to lecture me on the need to face someone when I'm speaking with them, or how to respect someone's personal space."

"Yes, I can understand that," Miss Audra said. "On the other hand, Natalie, I have actually known people who lost their sight after years of having it who needed to be reminded about how to start a conversation, and how to know when to laugh at a joke. Without being able to see, it's more difficult to pick up these social cues. All of us are just trying to prepare you. Ms. Kravitz is only doing her job."

"But even if I lost my sight, Miss Audra, it wouldn't turn me into an idiot."

"Well, that's a little harsh, Natalie, because you know blind people aren't idiots."

Natalie winced. "That's not what I meant."

"But that's what you implied," Miss Audra said.

"Sorry. I didn't mean it that way."

"Be careful what you say then. And remember, sometimes you just have to go with the program here. Try not to take everything so personally.

"You're a very bright young lady, Natalie. Just look at what you've accomplished these past two weeks."

"Yeah! I nearly killed myself falling down the stairs!"

"Well, there was that. But now that you're using the cane you'll be a lot safer. Once you put your mind to it, you'll pick up the technique very quickly. In fact, I'd like you to try to earn the Forestville Pass."

"The Forestville Pass?"

"Yes, you earn this pass by learning to walk a mile from school down Dunbar Avenue to the shopping center. There's an intersection with a traffic light and several other streets to cross. Once you have the pass, you're free to visit the shopping center on your own, whenever you like in your free time."

"A whole mile?" Natalie asked doubtfully. "Alone?"

"Yes."

Now that she thought about it, there weren't many times when Natalie was ever truly alone. It seemed she was always with someone—at school, in the car, in the house, in the barn. Had it always been that way?

But alone in Baltimore? Walking to a shopping center? What if she got lost? What if someone was mean to her? What if someone tried to steal her pocketbook or make her get into a car? It seemed crazy and irresponsible for Miss Audra to even suggest it.

"I'd be too afraid," she told Miss Audra. And that was the truth. The absolute rock-bottom truth.

"Trust me, it's not as hard as you think," Miss Audra told her.

Natalie turned away. Easy for her to say, she thought.

"Really, Natalie." Miss Audra's voice seemed so matter-of-fact. "You can't live in fear the rest of your life."

A DEAL WITH GOD

I . . . hear . . . the . . . " Natalie read slowly, moving her fingertips at a snail's pace across the workbook's bumpy Braille. It was still an incredible challenge. But the amazing thing? It was actually starting to make some sense. "M . . . u . . . mu . . . s. Music! I hear the music!"

"Good!" Miss Karen exclaimed.

Natalie pulled her hands back. "But look how slow I'm going," she said. "I mean, I could never read an entire book like this."

"Oh, but you will!" Miss Karen assured her. "Eve is reading one of the Harry Potter books right now. In fact, she left it on my desk." Miss Karen turned around to retrieve the book and put it in Natalie's hands.

"Whoa!" Natalie exclaimed, setting it down because it was so heavy. "Which story is this?" she asked. She'd read the entire series herself, using her magnifier the entire way.

"See if you can read the title," Miss Audra said.

Natalie sat up and positioned both hands on the cover. Slowly, she moved her fingertips forward. "The . . . o . . . r"—the *r* was easy because it actually looked liked an *r*—" . . . d . . . ord. Order! *The Order of the Phoenix!*"

"Right, but just the first volume," Miss Karen said. "The entire story is actually thirteen volumes in Braille."

Natalie was stunned, and awed by the thought of wading through that enormous ocean of bumps for pleasure. How could anyone? And yet—she looked up—Miss Karen, who sat across from her, knew Braille so well she could read it upside down, while facing Natalie.

"I don't understand," Natalie said. "How in the world do you do it?"

"Do *what*, Natalie?"

"Everything. I mean, not just the Braille. But you went to college. And now you ride two different buses and walk a whole mile by yourself to get to work every day. You make it seem so easy."

Miss Karen made a funny noise—like a snort? "I don't know about the easy part," she said. "Gosh, how do I do it? Long story, but I'll make it short.

"Like you, Natalie, I had vision when I was younger, but I was born with retinitis pigmentosis. It's a hereditary disease. My grandmother had it, my aunt has it, but my sister never got it. Where is the justice, right? When I was fifteen I lost everything. I was in high school then and, boy, what a difficult time that was. More difficult in some ways than my life now."

"*More* difficult? What do you mean?" Natalie asked.

"Because I felt as though I lived between two worlds. I went to a high school where, basically, I knew my way around and not everyone knew I was losing my sight. I used to sit in class and pray that no one would call on me to read. I needed large-print everything, but I didn't want the kids to see my large-print books, so I didn't even take them out of my backpack. I'd lie and say I forgot them. Then, of course, it was hard getting through the hallways if I didn't have a friend with me. I could have asked to leave class early in order to avoid those crowded halls, but I didn't want to stand out."

Exactly. It's how Natalie felt! It's why she had used her friends to get around, too. Even now, she didn't plan to use a cane when she returned to Western Allegany High. She didn't want to become known as "the blind girl." Most of the kids didn't even know she had a vision problem.

"I remember," Miss Karen went on, "how at lunch or in study hall, or if I was outside waiting for my mom to pick me up, I pretended that I was just looking down reading so I'd have an excuse for not seeing someone.

"I wasted so much time pretending," she said. "I just decided one day I wasn't going to live that way anymore. I mean this when I say it, Natalie." Miss Karen leaned forward and placed a hand on Natalie's, which rested on the Braille book between them. "It is easier to be blind than to pretend you're *not* blind."

At Teen Group that afternoon, the students talked about activities they might do together, including ice-skating, windsurfing, hiking, bowling, and sailing on a skipjack in the Chesapeake Bay. Natalie sat silently, wondering how in the world they could bowl if they couldn't see the pins. And ice-skating? Yikes. Yet these were activities that the kids routinely did, year after year. It confused Natalie—she would have to find an excuse not to go—and added a whole new layer of fear to the one she was already tamping down.

After burgers and boxed drinks, the kids split up into small groups to play UNO. Even Bree sat in on a game, with a little help from Sheldon on reading the Braille labels on each card. Natalie was glad that Bree was slowly becoming part of the group. Back in their dorm room, Natalie and Bree often talked, comparing notes on teachers (Miss Karen was awesome, they both agreed; Mr. Joe in American government was tough, but smart—and really cute, too); the music they enjoyed (Bree loved hip-hop and rap while Natalie was a shameless country fan); and food in the dining hall (the school's chicken anything was gross, no question about it, but they loved the tacos and the macaroni and cheese). One evening, Bree asked Natalie about the framed pictures on the wide bureau top they shared. "Can you tell me who is in them?"

"Sure," Natalie said. She knew the pictures by heart. "The biggest one is of my mom, dad, and me at my Honor Society induction. And then there's one of my best friend, Meredith, and me dressed like cats for Halloween. The picture in the sparkly frame is of my pet goat, Nuisance, and—"

"Your goat?" Bree laughed, interrupting. "You're serious? You have a goat?"

"I live on a goat farm."

"Awww. Do they have names?"

"Wow. We have about eighty goats now. They don't all have names, but some of the older ones do. Let's see, there's Jasmine, she was one of the first goats we owned. Then there's Morning Dew, Tootsie, Joy and Jess, Lacy, Crayola, Lazy Bones. Our two bucks are Bucky and Buddy."

"Do you mean billy goats?"

"Actually, male goats are bucks, not billys. Everybody thinks the females are called nanny goats, but they're not. They're does, like deer."

"Are they nice, Natalie?" Bree asked. "Are the goats friendly?"

"*Very* friendly. The only thing a goat loves more than another goat is a person. They hate being alone. They're very curious and very smart, too."

There was a pause.

"I don't have any pictures with me," Bree said. "Why would I, right? But if I did, I would have a picture of my aunt, because she has taken care of me ever since I was ten. That was about a year before my mother died. And I would have a picture of my boyfriend, Kirk. I don't really have any friends."

Natalie wondered what she meant by that. "But you have Kirk," she said. "You're lucky. I've never had a boyfriend."

"Well. I don't know if I'm so lucky. I think he sticks around out of pity more than anything else. I'm sure he blames himself for the accident."

"A car accident?" Natalie asked gently.

But Bree didn't answer. She rolled over on her bed and didn't say another word. Natalie let the question drop and went to brush her teeth.

There was a lot to think about on the long bus ride home. The week behind her, the weekend coming up at home. She would run her secret vision test in the morning, but Natalie didn't think things had worsened. As long as she had that tiny, precious, sliver of sight, she could get by. She even thought she could make a deal with God about this and, while the bus groaned its way over one of the steepest mountains toward the end of the trip, Natalie squeezed her eyes shut, pressed her hands together in her lap, and implored silently: *Let me keep what I have and I promise to have a good attitude. I will learn what I have to and I will help others.*

In the morning, the window test confirmed her vision hadn't changed, and Natalie figured that maybe God was listening. Maybe there *would* be a deal. Buoyed by the thought—and the fact that her shoulder felt so much better she didn't need the sling—Natalie rushed downstairs, hoping it wasn't too late to accompany her mother to the farmers' market.

Her mother was glad for the help. "What about your cane?" she asked as she stood by the kitchen door, waiting for Natalie to put on her hat.

"Don't need it," Natalie replied crisply.

"Really? Even after the fall at school?"

"Mom! I don't need it here!" she shot back, knowing full well she probably did. She added softly. "I just don't want people seeing it. Not yet."

Her mother didn't say anything more. But sitting in the front seat of the van a few minutes later, Natalie could feel her mother's disapproval. All Natalie would do at the market was put cheese into plastic bags and stuff in a flyer. Why would her mother care if Natalie had her cane or not?

After arriving at the market, they set up a folding table and two chairs at the back of the van. Then, before the first customers arrived, Natalie's mother dashed off to trade goat cheese for an Amish apple pie.

While she was gone, a familiar voice said, "Hello."

Startled, Natalie turned toward the voice.

"It's Jake Handelman—from school."

Still unable to see him, Natalie continued, bravely, to look in the direction of his voice and greeted him warmly. "Hi!"

"So how's it going?"

"Good," she told him. She hoped to high heaven she was looking in his direction. "How about you?"

"Fine, I guess. Heavy workload this year."

Finally, yes, she was able to glimpse part of him. She *was* looking at him. "Me too. A lot of homework."

"What are you taking?"

"Oh—let's see, I'm taking American government—and English—we're doing Shakespeare!" She hoped that would suffice. She certainly didn't want to mention the Braille, or Orientation and Mobility, and her dreaded meetings with a social worker.

"Cool," Jake replied. "Do you come home every weekend?"

Natalie nodded. "Yes. Every weekend."

"Well, heck. There's a football game tonight. I still play in the band. Are you coming? I have my license now. I could pick you up."

Pick her up? That sounded like a date!

"That's really nice of you," Natalie began. *But a football game at night? No way!* "I can't," she told him. "Not this weekend."

"Oh. Okay. Well, maybe another time."

"Sure, that'd be fun," Natalie agreed, although she knew she didn't mean it. It would be terribly awkward. And she would be terrified.

"Take care, Nat."

She smiled. "See ya."

Jake Handelman had asked her to go to the football game, right? Maybe. Or maybe he was just being nice. She wondered how Meredith would assess the situation. Thank goodness Jake hadn't wanted to buy any cheese, she thought. She wouldn't have been able to deal with the money. It would have been so embarrassing. Miss Karen's words walked out and stood in front of her, like little protestors in her own mind, waving signs: IT IS EASIER TO BE BLIND THAN TO PRETEND YOU'RE NOT BLIND. Angry, Natalie shook her head and knocked the little protestors out of her mind. She readjusted the brim of her hat and tightened the elastic in her ponytail. *Living between two worlds.* She pressed her lips together. Where in the devil was her mother? What was taking her so long?

Later in the morning, Professor Brodsky from Frostburg University stopped by. Natalie had helped in his campaign for state senator during the summer. She stood to shake hands with him and listened as he tried to convince her mother to sign a petition banning wind-power turbines in state parks. "I'm not against wind power now, don't get me wrong," he pointed out. "I just don't want to see those huge turbines spoiling the view of our western Maryland mountaintops. You know what I mean, Jean."

Natalie's mother signed the petition, but Natalie wasn't old enough.

"Stay in touch with me," the professor told Natalie. He touched her shoulder. "After I'm elected, I'm going to need some good interns the next couple years in Annapolis, where the state legislature meets."

Natalie smiled at his optimism—and his offer—but swallowed hard.

"I guess he doesn't know about my sight," she said to her mother after he had left.

"Not true. Dad and I saw him at the firehouse barbecue. He knows."

"He does?"

"All about it," her mother confirmed.

Sunday morning came way too fast. The only bright spot was that Meredith was expected for blueberry pancakes. Natalie was hoping there would be time for a short walk, even just out to the barn, so she could tell Meredith about the cane and her roommate, about running into Jake at the farmers' market—and about Arnab and how he always found a seat on the bus next to hers. Along about eleven o'clock, however, the phone rang. Meredith had overslept.

"Nat, I'm really sorry," she apologized. "I should have told my mom to get me up. Now I have to get ready. This guy, Richard, is coming."

"Richard? Who's Richard?"

"This kid at school. He's nice. Yeah. Anyway, a bunch of us are going down to the lake. They have a boat rental for noon."

"Oh."

"I'm so sorry, Nat. If I hadn't overslept, we would have had more time together. It is totally my fault."

It *was* Meredith's fault. But what was Natalie supposed to do about it? Make her feel guilty for having a real date with a boy?

On the bus, on the way back to school, Natalie took the HOPE stone out of her pocket and sat mindlessly rubbing it, and wondering if God took their deal seriously, while she stared out the bus window. Her view was nothing but a gray-green blur. But old habits died hard. If there was a window, you looked out.

She thought back to Miss Audra talking about clues and landmarks, how the landmarks were permanent, but how clues changed and couldn't be counted on. She guessed that, like clues, there were other things in her life she couldn't count on either.

PERSPECTIVE

Oddly, a group of adults was clustered outside of Natalie's room when she arrived back at school. As she and Serena walked wearily down the dormitory hall carrying their duffels and backpacks from the weekend at home, the evening counselor rushed forward to stop them.

"It's all right," the counselor assured the girls, nevertheless turning and guiding them back to the living room.

"What happened?" Natalie asked, glancing over her shoulder.

"Is it Gabriella?" Serena asked. "Did she try to commit suicide or something?"

There was an exasperated sigh. "No," the counselor said. "She did not try to commit suicide. I'll thank you to keep a lid on your comments, okay?

"Natalie," the counselor said, "I'm going to have you spend the night in Paula's room."

"Is Bree all right?" she asked.

"We'll explain later, okay?" was the response.

Another room? Without her things? Disappointed, Natalie turned, adjusted the duffel strap on her shoulder, and followed the dorm counselor. Paula was already in bed, propped up on pillows and listening to music on a CD player. Her wheelchair was parked against one wall, its large battery plugged into an outlet, charging up for the following day. Beside the bed, on the floor, was a large rubber mat with a set of clothes neatly laid out: shorts, T-shirt, underwear, and socks.

Paula pulled the earphones out of her ears. She tilted her head. "Welcome!" she said to Natalie.

"Thanks, Paula. Sorry to intrude on you like this."

"No, no. I'm glad to have you."

The counselor helped Natalie make up the extra bed with clean sheets and a blanket. Natalie then took her pajamas to the bathroom to change. When she came out, she heard a giggle and thought she saw Eve sitting on the end of Paula's bed with something on her lap.

"I've got cake," Eve whispered. "Leftovers from my brother's birthday."

"Is this the party?" Serena asked, coming in the door.

"Shhhhh!" Eve warned. Food was prohibited in the rooms.

Serena closed the door and Eve passed out chunks of cake on paper towels. Serena and Natalie sat cross-legged on the rubber mat beside the bed.

"So what do you think happened to Gabriella?" Eve asked.

"Bree. She likes to be called Bree," Natalie said, using a finger to scrape some of the frosting off her cake.

"Oh? I didn't know she had a nickname," Eve said.

"She should have told us," Paula added.

"I think she came back to school drunk," Serena declared.

Paula was shocked. "Oh, Lord!"

"She can get kicked out for that!" Eve said.

Natalie was skeptical. "Serena, how do you know she was drunk?"

"I don't! I'm just guessing," Serena said, shrugging. "And so what if she was? Haven't any of you guys been drunk before?"

Silence for a moment.

"No," Paula said.

"I had beer once," Eve added, "but I didn't get drunk."

"So what about you, Nat? You ever been drunk?" Serena giggled.

"No. Of course not."

"*Of course not!*" Serena echoed. "You're too perfect, you know that?"

Natalie did know it. Even her friends back at Western Allegany High kidded her about being perfect. But they didn't understand why Natalie skipped the Friday and Saturday night parties. She didn't stay home because she didn't want to drink. She didn't go because it was nighttime, and she couldn't *see*!

In the morning, Natalie was awakened by the jolt of Paula's alarm. Reaching over the desk beside her, Natalie pressed the button on her watch: *The time is . . . six . . . o'clock . . .* A.M.

Six o'clock? There was at least another hour to sleep.

"Sorry if I woke you," Paula apologized through the darkness.

"It's all right," Natalie replied, sleepy and confused.

There was not enough light in the room for Natalie to see, but she heard Paula roll off her bed and land on the mat with a heavy thump. The girl groaned and there were rubbing noises. Paula crawling? And Natalie realized that this must be her morning routine.

Slowly, Paula made her way across the room, disappearing into the bathroom. She didn't close the door, and Natalie could tell by the sounds that Paula had gotten herself up on the toilet and then flushed it. Natalie next heard water running. Had Paula managed to stand up at the sink? The sound of a washcloth dipped and wrung out in water, a sink emptying with a gurgle, and teeth being brushed confirmed it. A good thirty minutes had passed, Natalie guessed, when Paula crawled back toward her bed.

Natalie turned on the light, put on her glasses, and sat up. "Can I help you?" she asked.

"Oh, no, I'm fine," Paula replied. On all fours, and grunting with effort, Paula made it to the rubber mat and collapsed. After a couple deep breaths, she rolled over onto her back and began to dress. Which is why, Natalie realized, the clothes had been laid out the night before.

By seven fifteen, just as Paula was securing her leg braces with Velcro, Natalie was dressed, too. She finished packing up her books and sat on her bed, watching as Paula pulled herself up into the seat of her wheelchair.

"It's not fair," Natalie said.

"What?" Paula asked while still trying to catch her breath. "What's not fair?"

"That you have to be in a chair *and* that your eyesight is bad."

"But they're related, you know. The CP—the cerebral palsy—it affects my muscles, and we have muscles around our eyes, too. I do this every morning—unless my muscles lock up, then I need to wait for Miss Riley to come and get me undone. One night I got stuck behind the bed."

Slowly, Natalie shook her head. "You've got such a great attitude about it, Paula."

"Yeah. I try not to get down about it. I know that it's all how you look at it. Perspective! Ms. Kravitz says it's all about perspective—

that no matter how bad off you are, there's always somebody worse off than you. So be grateful. And I am. Still, sometimes I get the blues. I call it my blue funk."

Just then, an aide knocked softly on the door and came in, greeting the girls. Natalie assumed it must be Miss Riley, Paula's aide. The woman checked to see that Paula was buckled in properly and then unplugged the wheelchair's battery from the wall. "All set?" she asked.

"All set!" Paula replied. She pushed the joystick with her right hand and maneuvered the motorized wheelchair through the door.

"Natalie," Miss Riley said, "if you could just stay behind a second. I want to talk to you about your roommate."

"Is Bree okay?" Natalie asked.

"She had a seizure last night. That's why we wanted someone else to stay with her for the night. She has these seizures from time to time. They're from injuries related to her accident. We just wanted to tell you that. If you think she's having a seizure, you should get help immediately."

"How would I know she was having a seizure?" Natalie asked.

"You'd know; she kind of spaces out and shakes uncontrollably."

"Is there something I could do for her right away?"

"Sure. You could help her get down on the floor and loosen up any tight clothing near her neck. But most important, get some help."

"Of course," Natalie replied.

"Thanks, hon. Well, I'll let you get on your way to breakfast."

Natalie nodded, picked up her backpack and opened her cane. Feeling humbled, she left the room and followed Paula down the hall.

———

Later that day, in gym class, Mr. Lee added yet another thought about perspective.

"The number one reason people are victims is that they are nice!" the karate instructor declared. "They don't want to *offend* anyone! Everyone teaches children to be nice little girls and boys," he continued, his voice again echoing in the gym. "But this can get in the way of your intuition, your *gut feeling*. You need to pay attention to that gut feeling!"

He talked about setting boundaries. "Draw a circle around your personal space and make it clear that *this is your space*."

"Two ways you can do this," Mr. Lee told them. "Verbal and physical. Verbal means you say something. If someone takes your arm and wants to help you, poor blind person, across the street, but you don't want to cross the street, then you need to say loud and clear: 'Thank you, but I don't need your help.' If they don't let go, you have to be more forceful. Twist your arm away! Yell at them! 'Take your hands off! Let go of me!'

"Your voice is important," Mr. Lee emphasized. "Practice making your voice strong and loud. Yes. Nice little children are taught to be quiet and soft-spoken. But, blind people, it's important for you to use a strong voice."

"Okay!" He clapped his hands together. "Let's practice saying: 'Stop! Leave me alone!' Everyone!"

"Stop!" the girls shouted together. "Leave me alone!"

"Louder!" Mr. Lee cried. "I want you take in a big breath and push the words up from your belly! Again!"

"Stop! Leave me alone!" the girls hollered again, their voices filling the small gym and bouncing off the walls.

"Good! Now. What did the book say about telling a lie?" Mr. Lee asked.

Serena's hand flew up. "The book says it's okay for blind people to lie," she said.

A few of the girls chuckled.

"It's true." Serena went on to explain: "The book says that if you're, like, at a bus stop and a stranger asks if you can see faces, he may be trying to scope out if you're an easy hit. Like maybe you won't be able to recognize him later. But he could be a serial killer or a rapist or just some weirdo. Don't feel you have to answer somebody's dumb question with the truth, especially if the question, like, makes you uncomfortable."

"Excellent!" Mr. Lee exclaimed. "Pretty soon, we get physical!"

Things kind of fell into a routine about then. Bree seemed to be trying more, and Natalie wasn't quite as homesick, even if she still looked forward to daily phone calls to and from home.

"How's the cat?" she asked her mother one night. "Does he still wait outside the milk room for his scraps every morning?"

There was a pause.

"Actually, we haven't seen the cat for a while," her mother said. "But he's wild, Natalie. You know how they are."

Natalie was sad to hear the cat had disappeared.

"A guy caught a fifty-one-pound carp in Deep Creek Lake," her father suddenly recalled. He probably didn't want her moping about the cat. "Everyone's talking about that. Hey! And the Steelers won last night! I bet the kids were excited."

"Actually, Dad, the kids here are all Ravens fans," Natalie had to tell him. "Remember? Most of them live in Baltimore."

"Oh, gosh," he replied. He sounded disappointed.

Her mother jumped in next to report what the cousins were doing. "Uncle Jack says Florie and Tiffany helped tag monarch butterflies so scientists can track their flight to Mexico," she said. "Isn't that something? Those little things flying all that way?"

Then, midway through the week, there was a call from Meredith.

Meredith: *Nat, I wanted to tell you something really exciting. I've been asked to the homecoming dance this year—with a senior! Can you believe it?*

Natalie: *Homecoming. Wow, Meres, that's wonderful!* (Natalie forced herself to sound cheerful. She had never been to a formal dance herself.) *Who's taking you?*

Meredith: *That guy who took us to the lake last weekend, remember? Richard. Except everyone calls him Richie.*

Natalie: *Richie.*

Meredith: *Richie Mengler. He's on the basketball team. Maybe you can come to a game this winter if you get home early enough on Friday. Yeah. So it's exciting, but now I have to find a dress. There's got to be something out there that will look good on me.*

Natalie: *I'm sure you'll find the perfect dress.*

Meredith: *Look, I gotta go. Richie's calling at eight thirty and I need to get my homework done or Mom won't let me talk. See ya.*

There was a click and Meredith was gone.

"Thanks for calling," Natalie said sarcastically into the dead phone.

It was happening, wasn't it? Meredith was drifting away and there wasn't anything Natalie could do to stop it. She was having a normal life while Natalie was struggling to have a life, period. It wasn't anger Natalie felt right then, not even jealousy, just an enormous wistfulness. A sadness.

Bree, who sat on her bed practicing Braille, moved a piece of paper. Surely, she had heard. Out in the hall, a door closed and the sound of a cane hitting the wall echoed down the corridor.

"Hey, my aide gave me this book today," Bree said.

Natalie rolled her eyes. She was not in a mood to chitchat.

But Bree got up and started patting the top of her desk. "Here it is." She bumped into her chair, but walked across the room to Natalie and pushed the book into her hands. "You have a little magnifier thingee to read, don't you?"

"Bree, I need to be doing my homework—"

"Come on," Bree urged her. "My aide was reading this today and it was *really* corny, but funny, too. Just open to a random page and read it."

Natalie clicked on her light and focused on the title: *14,000 Things to Be Happy About.* She knew Bree was only trying to cheer her up because of the phone call. Opening to the middle of the book, she ran her finger down the page. A wan smile lifted the corners of her mouth. "Dogs nose-deep in wrapping paper," she read aloud. "An herb-stuffed pillow. Leisurely bubble baths. Slices of fresh pineapple. Bengay muscle rub."

"Oh, I hate that stuff!" Bree interrupted.

"Me too," Natalie agreed. Then she read the next one: "Walking into your dreams and coming out a new person . . ." And she stopped. "You know, I have that dream. I dream sometimes that I can still see as well as I did years ago. Like I'm running through the fields or chasing goats. I can see everything so clearly."

"You had good vision then?" Bree said.

"Pretty normal until I was about eight years old."

"Me too," Bree said. "I had perfect vision until the accident in June. Now I have nothing."

Natalie looked at her and saw that Bree was kind of hunched over on her bed, twisting strands of her long hair in her hands.

"I wanted to be a dancer," Bree said. "I took dancing lessons all my life. My mom was so proud of that. She's the one who started me out with tap dance lessons. It's like the one little dream I had: being a dancer. Then in one afternoon, one stupid thing and it's over."

"I'm so sorry," Natalie said quietly. "Sometimes I wonder which would be worse, losing vision slowly, like me—or all at once, like you."

"Yeah." Bree nodded. "I guess I know where the term *blindsided* came from. It might have been nice to get ready for this. It's been such a nightmare."

Natalie disagreed. "No," she said, "having time to get ready doesn't make it easier. No one can possibly be prepared to go blind."

Another moment passed when neither of them spoke.

"Guess I'll go ahead and wash up for bed and do my eyedrops," Natalie said. But walking across the room, she tripped over the balloon Meredith had given her. The helium was practically gone and the balloon hovered, an eerie metallic ghost, about an inch above the floor. Natalie reached down and grabbed it, then went to her desk for a pair of scissors, cut off its end, and stuffed the deflated balloon in the wastebasket.

No matter how bad off you are, there's always somebody worse off than you. So be grateful. . . . It was probably good advice repeating in Natalie's head. But right then, she wished she could have been one of those little butterflies flying to Mexico.

INTERSECTIONS

During the next few weeks at school, the weather shifted and the hot, humid days of summer were blown away by refreshing breezes that brought a stretch of pleasant fall days. Bright colors decked out the forest surrounding the campus, and while not even Natalie could fully appreciate the pretty foliage, all the kids enjoyed the crunchy sound their canes made sweeping aside leaves on the school's sidewalks. Time was passing; many of the major challenges of six weeks ago were now merely part of daily routine.

But time was running out, too. And Natalie knew it. Her tiny circle of vision had shrunk to the circumference of a drinking straw. Deep inside, she kept her fears at bay by living on hope and denial. Outwardly, Natalie was the star student, feverishly learning new skills, plunging forward, and keeping herself so busy there was never time for her to stop and examine reality, or poke at the fear that lay hidden beneath the surface. Busy. Keeping busy became her modus operandi.

Natalie spent hours in the library or hunched over her desk in her room, completing her lessons with the magnifier and pounding on the Brailler for practice. She stopped counting steps and focused exclusively on cane technique and memorizing mental maps of the school. In her room, Natalie no longer threw her cane in the back of the closet. She carefully set it on the shelf above her clothes, beside her umbrella. A "Go Cougars!" key chain and a simple, silver whistle had been attached to the cane's handle to identify it as hers.

In her frenetic race against time, Natalie took to heart every new skill she was taught. On laundry day, she did her own wash, using grippers to hold socks of the same color together. She kept herself organized by using different-shaped containers for shampoo, conditioner, and bath gel. A rubber band around her tube of face cream prevented Natalie from getting it mixed up with her toothpaste.

With others from the dorm, she used the George Foreman grill to turn out steak and chicken dinners. She shopped for groceries and discovered that there were employees available at some food stores who would assist with shopping. The girls then identified the food with premade Braille labels stuck on index cards that they rubber-banded around the boxes of food. A good idea, Natalie realized, since many food items—such as rice, cake mix, cornstarch, and brown sugar—came in similar-size boxes.

The fighting lessons were yet to come, but eagerly awaited. Natalie and the others giggled in the hallway one night, wondering which was better: gym class with Mr. Lee or their new health class every other week with Miss La Verne. The girls made Braille calendars to track their periods the first week. Next time, each of them made a fist-size uterus out of clay to get a tactile idea of what they carried inside their own bodies. They also created clay ovaries the size of grapes and connected the ovaries to the clay uterus with pipe cleaners that represented Fallopian tubes. There was a rumor that in an upcoming class a rubber penis would be passed around. . . .

Natalie also threw herself into doing things for others as well. (She hadn't forgotten her deal with God.) She talked about starting a student council for the kids at school and perhaps asking for Braille labels on the salad bar so everyone could make their own salad. She tried to think of ways in which the girls on her floor could have fun together in the evenings, too.

"Come on," Natalie begged Eve. "I know it sounds dumb but give it a chance. Bree said she'd watch the movie if everyone else did. Anything to get her off the cell phone with her boyfriend!"

"A descriptive movie. *Ugh*. Where some guy describes everything? I hate those. If it's stupid, Natalie, I'm leaving," Eve warned.

The girls put on their pajamas and slowly gathered in the living room, some bringing their pillows. Natalie popped popcorn in the microwave. When they were ready, Natalie pushed in the tape (amazingly, the school still had a VCR) and started the bowl of popcorn around.

"This better be R-rated," Serena said, still combing out wet hair from a shower.

The television screen flickered and a voice came on: *An animated logo appears in three-dimensional letters: FOX VIDEO . . . And now the screen glows an eerie blue, then fills with swirling white mist. We fly through the misty clouds. . . . The snow-covered Alps give way to a sunny Alpine meadow where a young woman with short blond hair strolls in the grass swinging her arms in a carefree stride. She wears black shoes and stockings and a gray striped apron over a black dress. She spreads her arms and twirls in a joyous spin as she bursts into song: "The hills are alive—"*

"With the SOUND OF MUSIC!" the girls all chimed in at the same time.

"Oh, come on, give me a break!" Serena moaned. "I am not watching *The Sound of Music*! It's for little kids."

"It is not! I love this movie!" Murph cried.

"Yeah, it's nice, Serena. Relax and enjoy it," Natalie said.

Which is exactly what they did. All of them. They stayed for the entire movie. And for two days following, sweet strains of "Edelweiss" could be heard, hummed and sung out loud in the hallways of that dorm.

Underneath it all, of course, the truth of what was happening stalked Natalie, like a beast in the bushes. When Natalie allowed herself to even *think* about the possibilities, even momentarily, the result was not just scary, it was crippling. Outwardly, she seemed to be doing well. Inwardly, she was still scared to death.

"I want to be a biker chick or a gangster's moll," Serena said casually at lunch one day.

"A *mall*?" Murph asked. "I thought that's where you went shopping."

"Wrong moll," Serena retorted. "This moll is like a gangster's mistress. You know, a prostitute? Do you need me to define that?"

"Noooo. Duh. I know what a prostitute is."

For the past few days, conversation at mealtime had pretty much centered around costumes for the school's annual Halloween party.

"I am going to be a pirate," Arnab told them. "With a patch over one eye."

"Better not put a patch over the other eye, too, or you won't be able to see," Sheldon joked.

"How about you, Natalie?" JJ asked. "What are you going to be?"

"Earth to Natalie," Serena said. "Are you coming?"

"Of course," Natalie forced herself to say as she went to work prying the top off a carton of yogurt. "Do you think I'd miss it? I was a cat last year." Her hands stopped moving as she recalled last year's Halloween sleepover at Meredith's. Coralee and Suzanne were there, too. Meredith had polished Natalie's nails while they watched a scary movie—the girls didn't mind filling Natalie in on what she couldn't see—and they didn't go to sleep until three o'clock in the morning.

"A cat?" Eve was asking. "Did you say a cat?"

"Yes, a cat," Natalie said. "If I can find my tail and my ears."

"Don't you hate that? I am always misplacing my tail and ears," Serena quipped.

"Don't you mean your tail and your *horns*?" Sheldon deadpanned.

The kids laughed, glad that Sheldon had gotten in the last word for once. But Natalie sat quietly with the yogurt container still unopened in front of her.

Miss Audra knew something was bothering Natalie. "Are things at home okay?" she asked. "That good friend of yours—Meredith?"

Natalie picked up her folded cane from the floor. "Meredith has a boyfriend now, so I don't see much of her," she said. "Between Richie and driver's ed and getting ready for Homecoming, she's pretty busy." She turned toward her cane instructor and smiled ever so slightly. "Miss Audra, isn't it Ms. Kravitz's job to pry into my personal life?"

"I'm sorry, Nat. I didn't mean to pry," she said, "but I need your full attention today, because you're going all the way to the traffic light."

Down the hallway, Natalie focused as she swept her cane side to side in a perfect arc. Outside, Natalie moved her cane against the grass that grew along the sidewalk—shorelining, they called it—and made her way to the big bush, where she turned right and shorelined her way to Nader Lane.

"Are you listening?" Miss Audra asked. "Tell me what you hear."

Natalie stopped. "A lawn mower," she said. "Off to the right, on the hillside. Children playing." She pointed with her left hand. "There, at the nursery school." Natalie lifted her chin. "And traffic moving."

"Is it close?" Miss Audra asked.

Natalie shook her head. "No. It's up ahead."

"Excellent."

When Natalie's cane detected the beginning of a sidewalk to her left, she turned, knowing the walk ran west along Dunbar Avenue. Traffic on Dunbar was steady and brisk. Soon Natalie's cane hit a metal pole. Vehicles converged from all sides. "We're at the traffic light," she said.

"Are you sure?" Miss Audra asked. "Maybe it's just a stop sign."

"No. Because if it was a stop sign the pole would feel different— skinnier—and cars would be stopping briefly, before moving on."

"Good. This *is* the traffic light," Miss Audra confirmed. "What's the first thing you're going to do here?"

"Listen," Natalie replied. "When traffic directly in front of me has stopped, and when the traffic to my right moves, it's my signal to cross."

"Right."

But there was no way Natalie was going to cross that street. Not today. Not tomorrow. Not next week. Not ever. "Is it okay if we go back now?"

"Absolutely, Natalie. You did a great job coming this far. But next time, Natalie, I do expect you to cross."

"Yes, I'll try," Natalie assured her. But only to please Miss Audra.

"You can do it," her instructor insisted. "You're going to come to a lot of intersections in your life, Natalie, roads and otherwise, and you can't always just turn around. You have to summon the courage to go forward."

Natalie nodded again. "I understand." She was a good student after all. And an excellent faker.

A couple days later, Teen Group piled into three different vans and took a field trip to BISM, which stood for Blind Industries and Services of Maryland. At BISM, blind people worked in a huge warehouse mixing chemicals for cleaning supplies. Other blind workers operated machines that cut out thousands of pieces of camouflage material, which were stacked, wrapped, and sent to federal prisons for inmates to sew into U.S. military uniforms. Blind people there also put together office materials for state government employees, and taught classes in cooking, wood shop, and computer technology for other blind people.

When the kids returned to school, Natalie found herself walking up the hill toward the dorms beside Arnab.

"I found that a bit depressing," he confided as they trailed slightly behind the rest of the group. He paused, waiting for Natalie, and they walked slowly, careful not to let their canes get tangled up.

"Me too," Natalie agreed. "I wouldn't want to be working one of those jobs. I mean I know they're important jobs for a lot of people, but—"

"So boring," Arnab said.

"Totally."

"Have you thought—what you will do in *your* life?" Arnab asked her.

"I always thought I'd go to college, but I'm not so sure now.

If I do, though—well, I've always been interested in government. I volunteered for a professor running for the state senate and I admired what he did. He knocked on people's doors and talked to them about issues."

"Ah. A politician!" Arnab said with a lilt in his voice.

"Well, there are *some* good politicians," Natalie insisted. "I mean they *can* help people."

"Yes, yes."

"Anyway," Natalie said, "it's just a silly dream."

"No, no, not silly," Arnab said. "Our dreams, they keep us going."

When they reached the top of the hill, the sidewalk split, with one pathway leading downhill to the boys' dorm, the other to the girls' residence. There was a bench and Arnab suggested they sit for a moment.

"Sure," Natalie replied, taking a seat and folding her cane. "What about you? What do you think you'll do, Arnab?"

"I have always wanted to be a land use planner," he said.

"What's that?" Natalie asked.

"Someone who plans how and where we will build our houses and our cities in the future. My father does this. He is a research scientist at the National Center for Smart Growth, at the University."

"Oh, I see."

A breeze came through, knocking ropes against the flagpole nearby and sending dried leaves tumbling down the sidewalk and against their legs and feet. The air smelled moist, like rain, Natalie noticed.

"What do you miss most?" Natalie asked Arnab.

"Color," Arnab answered without hesitation. "Seeing colors. . . ."

"Yeah. That's a big one all right," Natalie agreed. "You have no sight at all then?"

He shook his head. "No. Nothing."

A short moment passed.

"I wonder sometimes," Arnab said, breaking the silence, "what color are your eyes, Natalie?"

She grinned. "My eyes? Well, I don't have an iris, so I guess the answer is no color at all. Although I do have a pupil that's large and black. So maybe you'd say I have two black eyes."

Arnab didn't laugh. "You don't have an iris?"

"No. I was born without them. You know what the iris does, right?"

"Yes, yes. The iris controls the amount of light that enters the eye."

"Since I don't have an iris, bright light really bothers me, which is why I always have a hat on, and my tinted glasses."

Arnab reached over to touch her head. "Ah! I forgot!"

"It gets complicated," she said, "but basically that's how I developed juvenile glaucoma."

"I see. Well . . . I don't see." He laughed nervously. "But I do understand."

Another brief moment passed when neither one of them spoke. Then Arnab cleared his voice. "Natalie," he began, his voice slightly different, "I wondered if I could ask you something."

"Sure," she said.

"I wondered, do you think it might be okay—if I touched your face?"

Natalie turned to him. She couldn't see him very clearly, but she thought he was looking down, with his good hand gripping one knee. And she knew it had taken a lot of courage to ask.

"My hands are clean," Arnab said. "Mr. Joe said it's important that your hands are clean."

Natalie's heart dipped. She smiled. "Yes," she said. "It would be okay."

Arnab sat up. Turning slightly toward her, he lifted his right hand and put it on Natalie's arm.

Natalie helped guide his hand to her face, then took her own hand away and remained still—so still she didn't even breathe.

Gently, very gently, Arnab's fingers moved across her forehead. He felt the bill of her cap and chuckled softly.

"I told you," Natalie said.

His fingertips, light as feathers, traced her brows, then brushed one cheek and, crossing her nose, moved up and down slowly to explore the other cheek. He took his hand off her face momentarily, but returned with slightly trembling fingers to trace the outline of her chin, and finally, her lips.

He brought his hand away and sighed.

Natalie wondered what he was thinking, what he expected and what he had found.

"I was right," Arnab said.

"You were right?"

"Yes, yes. I knew that you were very beautiful."

"But how can you tell?" Natalie asked in a nervous, joking way. No boy had ever told her she was beautiful. Not ever. Nor had anyone ever touched her this way.

"I can tell," he said.

A lump rose in Natalie's throat. "Thank you," she whispered. Then, summoning her own courage, she reached over and gently squeezed his hand.

AN ORDINARY MORNING

For two evenings in a row, Natalie took the framed photographs from her bureau and sat, cross-legged on her bed, with the pictures spread out before her. With her lighted magnifier, she memorized every feature in the images by staring, with what minuscule amount of vision remained, until each line, each shadow, each nuance of color was etched in her mind. Not just the proud, happy faces of her parents, but the way her father's long fingers grasped the narrow shoulders of both her and her mother the night of the Honor Society induction. Gazing at the picture of Nuisance, Natalie thought of how many times she had stroked the long, luxurious white ears on that silky brown goat. Ears, she once thought, that resembled enormous tongues. Ears so long that Natalie had actually seen them blow in the wind.

As she compiled her mental scrapbook, a vague uneasiness gnawed at her insides and a corner of her heart felt pinched. Natalie knew she was preparing herself. If hope was a flame, it was flickering on a short wick.

And still—*still* it came as a whopping surprise. A shock, really, to awaken one Wednesday, an ordinary morning in the middle of November, only to see a solid sheet of—not foreboding blackness— but indecisive gray. A massive, ethereal gray screen, up close, with tiny, flickering splotches of light.

Natalie blinked. Several times she blinked, and rubbed her eyes hard with the palms of her hands, trying to clear her tiny window into the world. But nothing changed. She sat up and turned her head from side to side as though that would shake it loose, but nothing changed. Her heart began to beat faster; she could feel the rapid thumping in her chest, and the tightening of her throat.

Across the hall, Eve's Carolina wren on the bird clock sang at 7 A.M. When her own alarm went off, Natalie reached over to turn it off, scooped up the pink HOPE stone that she regularly left on the desk beside her at night. Scared, squeezing the stone in one hand, she lay back down, pulling, with a trembling grip, the sheets up to her chin. She clenched her eyes shut and yearned desperately to go back in time, holding her breath until it hurt and she had to breathe again.

Was this it? Would her sight come back later in the day? In the week? She already knew that even on the darkest of days, she would have hope.

Did she need to call the doctor? Her parents? What should she do, she wondered. Tears collected and began to trickle down her cheeks.

And where was God? What happened to the deal? Why did he let her down? If it had to happen, why did it have to happen at school, where she was so far away from home? Maybe there was no God! Because if there really was a God, why would he do this to her?

Bree heard the sniffling, and when the sniffling became sobs, she seemed to know instantly what had happened overnight while both of them had slept peacefully and unaware. She took a seat on the edge of Natalie's bed and, without a word, reached over and gently took Natalie's hands away from her face and held them in her own. She leaned in, her forehead touching the top of Natalie's head, still saying nothing, just letting Natalie know—as only another blind person could—that she was not alone.

"DON'T STAY THERE"

Word spread quickly. Natalie could hear the quiet voices in the hall. Eve came to give her a hug and Serena stopped by the door to say she was sorry. Bree even offered to stay with her, but the day counselor said all the girls needed to go to class.

"Have you called your parents?" the woman asked, after placing a cup of coffee in Natalie's hands. Natalie didn't drink coffee, but she took it anyway.

"Yes," replied Natalie, who was still sitting on her bed. Just sitting, with her back against the wall. Out of habit, she wore her tinted glasses and her Cougars cap, not even knowing for sure whether the light would bother her, now that she was officially blind.

Odd that there was no pain, she thought. The transition from sight to blindness would be mentally and emotionally wrenching, but the pure physical fact of it had been silent and painless.

"You talked with them—your parents?" The question was repeated.

Natalie nodded numbly.

The counselor stood for a moment. She was close to the bed, and smelled faintly of perspiration and flowery cologne. "Is there anything else I can do?" she asked.

Natalie shook her head.

"Well. Here's a muffin for you, too, hon. It's there, on a napkin to your right."

"Thank you," Natalie mumbled. For some reason she had a flashback to the school's Halloween party, how one of the refreshments set out was a tray of "Halloween Eyes"—rounds of cucumber with a squirt of sour cream and a thin slice of green olive for the iris. The iris that Natalie didn't have.

"I know Miss Karen is on her way over to see you."

Natalie didn't say anything, just leaned forward to set the coffee on the corner of her desk.

A few moments later, she heard the Braille instructor and her guide dog approaching the room. Herky's dog tags jingled and his toenails clicked on the tiled hallway. They paused at the doorway. "Natalie, it's Miss Karen. May I come in?"

"Of course," Natalie said. "There is a chair at my desk, Miss Karen. When you come in, it's to your right."

"Thank you," Miss Karen said. She sat, and Natalie could hear Herky plop down on the floor beside her. She didn't have to see the dog to know that he rested his head on his paws, eyes alert.

"You know that I went through this myself when I was fifteen years old," Miss Karen said to Natalie.

"Yes. You told me," Natalie said, feeling as if her comments were on automatic pilot this morning. Nothing Miss Karen could say was going to make her feel any better. Nothing anybody could say would make it better.

"A lot of people will tell you how sorry they are that you have lost your sight, Natalie. I am one of them. It's an enormous loss, there's no question. . . . You know how much I'd like to see that digital display on my bread maker."

The corners of Natalie's mouth lifted slightly.

"But I am not going to get all emotional about it," Miss Karen went on. "There is one thing I want to tell you though—and I hope you'll think about it. It is this: acknowledge the loss. But don't stay there."

All morning, different people came and went. Natalie figured they didn't want her to be alone. She was glad no one forced her to go to class. It was like a sick day, but worse—so much worse.

Before too long, Miss Audra came, and Natalie stood for the embrace she knew would come from her cane instructor. When Natalie hugged her, she felt the long braid down Miss Audra's back.

"I'm going to take you to see the school's doctor on call," she said. "Dr. Leanders said she would stop by this morning."

"Why?" Natalie asked. "What can she do?"

"Probably nothing for your sight. But what she can do is check the pressure and adjust your eyedrops. You don't want to damage your eyes."

Natalie wondered what difference it would make if her eyes got damaged now. But the doctor took a look anyway, and, just as Miss Audra predicted, adjusted the eyedrops to bring the pressure down. She did not give Natalie hope that things would change. "I'm sorry," she said when the exam was over.

Sorry. Was that it? Was that all she was going to say?

No. There was more. "You should see your own doctor within the month."

When they returned to Natalie's room, Miss Audra left Natalie with a bag of peanut M&M's (a consolation prize?) and the reminder that they would walk to the Forestville Shopping Center on their first lesson following the Thanksgiving break. "What do you say? Let's celebrate with pizza at the Parthenon. Arnab is taking the test with his instructor, too. We can meet at the restaurant and eat together."

Did Natalie ever respond? She couldn't remember.

Midway through the afternoon, Natalie heard familiar voices in the hall. Her parents! Why hadn't someone told her they were coming? She rose quickly and walked partway across the room, opening her arms and letting her mother rush into them.

Her father embraced her, too, and for a moment the three of them stood, clinging to one another. Just knowing they had left the farm and made whatever enormous arrangements they had to make for the goats—then driven five hours to get to the school—made Natalie cry all over again.

"We've come to take you home," her father said.

"If that's what you want," her mother quickly added.

"We can pack you up and have you out of here in twenty minutes," her father said.

It caught Natalie off guard. She sniffed and wiped at her cheeks. "I have an exam tomorrow—" she started to say.

"Who cares?" her father said.

"And we're going out for sundaes because it's Serena's birthday. . . ."

Her father grunted.

"It's Natalie's decision," her mother said firmly.

"Who's taking care of the goats?" Natalie asked, steering them away, if only momentarily, from the subject at hand.

"Uncle Jack," her father said. "He said he'd stay the night in case we didn't make it back."

Natalie knew this was a huge inconvenience for them.

The counselor returned and suggested the family get out of the dorm and go somewhere together for a while.

"We don't know Baltimore," Natalie's mother said. "What do you suggest?"

"Oh, gosh. Well. You could go down to the Inner Harbor. All kinds of things there: paddleboats, restaurants, gift shops, the aquarium. There's even a carousel to ride up by the Science Center."

What a waste of time and energy, Natalie thought. If she couldn't see, why would she want to ride around in a paddleboat? Or go up and down in a circle on a wooden horse? If she couldn't see the fish, why would she want to go to the aquarium?

"I think it's a great idea," her mother said, surprising Natalie. "Let's get directions and go."

Instead, they got lost. A gas station attendant in a place called White Marsh gave them new directions, but Natalie could feel the frustration growing. They weren't talking about anything—least of all Natalie's blindness. It was almost as though they were driving around to avoid it. Plus it was hot in the car. Plus she couldn't see anything. . . .

"Can't we just stop somewhere?" Natalie pleaded.

"Sure. Of course we can. How about an early dinner?" her mother suggested. "We never did have lunch. Did we, Frank?"

They stopped at a diner. "Home-cooked food," Natalie's mother said, reading an outdoor sign.

Natalie didn't have much of an appetite, but again, that wasn't really the point. She held her mother's arm, but used her cane, too, to make her way into the diner and slide to an inside seat at one of the booths. Her mother squeezed in beside her.

When the waitress brought glasses of water, Natalie blurted: "Do you have a Braille menu?" But why did she do that? She probably couldn't even read it.

"I'm sorry," the waitress said. "We don't."

"That's fine," her mother rushed to reassure everyone. "I can just read everything to her."

She had probably embarrassed her parents, Natalie thought. Especially her father, who had grown so quiet. He would have to finally accept the fact that she couldn't see now, wouldn't he? Her poor father. Tears sprang into her eyes. Natalie felt herself shrinking backward into the booth.

Her mother began reading from the menu: "They serve breakfast all day, Nat. There's French toast, pancakes, omelets—"

"An omelet," Natalie said to stop her. "A cheese omelet."

"Okay."

The waitress returned to take orders, but Natalie's mother still needed a second, so Natalie's dad ordered first. "I'll try your liver and onions," he said. "Comes with mashed potatoes, right?"

Natalie's mother ordered a BLT.

"And what about her?" the waitress asked. "What will she have?"

What? Was she a child now? Now that she was blind? Miss Karen's words echoed in her head: *Don't stay there.* Natalie knew she should sit up and assert herself by placing her own order. But she remained, stolid, in her slumped position in a corner of the booth, her face tilted down, the folded cane on the seat beside her.

When the waitress brought their food, Natalie's mother put an arm around her shoulders and asked if there was anything she could do.

Natalie stared into the gray wall that was her world now and remembered something from an earlier meal in the dormitory kitchen.

Her mother squeezed her shoulders.

"Look at my plate, Mom," Natalie said.

"Okay. I'm looking at it."

"If my plate was a clock, what would be at twelve o'clock?"

"A clock . . ." her mother repeated softly, at first confused. "Oh—well, the toast is at twelve o'clock, Nat. There are some hash browns at three o'clock. The omelet is at six o'clock, and you've got a couple orange slices there at nine."

"Thanks," Natalie said. She sat up, put the napkin in her lap, and found her fork. Advice from the first few days of school—ignored then, but stored away—suddenly came to mind: *Mashed potatoes and toast make good "bumpers" because you can push your food against them. . . . Remember to* stab *your food, so it doesn't fall off the fork.*

There was a lot to learn. For all of them.

SEEING IS BELIEVING

The next morning, Natalie regretted not returning home with her parents. She would have to force herself to get through the next couple days, she figured, maneuvering her cane through the hallway to her first period class. Heck, she would have to force herself to get through life, because how could anything be fun anymore?

"A federal appeals court has ruled that the U.S. currency system discriminates against blind people," Mr. Joe told the students when they had taken their seats. "They say it discriminates because all paper money feels the same. In Canada, paper money has embossed dots that vary by denomination. And the euro—the currency used in Europe—has a foil feature so you can feel the difference in bills.

"Here is your assignment for the Thanksgiving break," he continued. "I want you to examine both sides of this issue. Should the American government—and our businesses—change the shape and feel of our U.S. currency to help people who can't see? Why or why not?"

"Of course they should change our money. It's not fair!" Murph blurted loudly.

"That's what the American Council of the Blind said!" Mr. Joe exclaimed. "They're the ones who filed a suit over seven years ago—and the court agreed. The court ruled that the current system violates the federal Rehabilitation Act, which does what? Sheldon, go ahead,"

"The Rehabilitation Act is intended to ensure that people with disabilities can fully participate in society."

"Correct," Mr. Joe noted. "But the U.S. Treasury says blind people can simply use credit cards instead of cash. What's more, they said, changing the size of our bills will force companies to spend *billions of dollars* to redesign their vending machines."

Serena didn't wait for Mr. Joe to call on her. "Yeah, but not everything can be paid for with a credit card," she pointed out. "And besides, I'm not old enough to have one!"

"Okay," Mr. Joe said. "Eve, did you want to add something?"

"Yes. If someone gives me change, like in a store? I have to have faith that it's the right amount. That or else I have to ask a stranger for help and I shouldn't have to do that."

"All right, guys! These are all good arguments. Save them for your papers! I want at least two pages supporting your position. Go online to gather your research. You've got two more days at school, so if you need to use the computers here, do so before you leave."

Natalie sat quietly, listening but not participating, and not taking much interest in class other than to think that the money thing would just be one more hassle she would have to deal with now.

On the bus heading home for the Thanksgiving break, Natalie reflected on how, through the dreary darkness of the past two days, her friends at school had been a bright spot. Serena had even urged her to join the swim team, or be a cheerleader for the wrestling team that started practice in a week. Eve helped her gather information for the American government paper online with the talking JAWS computer program. And Bree had been eager to both listen and talk. Natalie's loss of sight, it seemed, had brought them all closer.

"You'll be glad to know I'm taking my cane home," Bree had told Natalie before the buses came. "So you don't have to remind me this time. I'm *using* it, too. Despite what my boyfriend thinks." Natalie put on a happy face and embraced her. "Good luck," she said.

Arnab tried to comfort Natalie as well. After Teen Group, he sought her out. "After my accident," he confided, "I was very depressed when I awoke in the hospital and could see nothing. My father said to me, 'Arnab, you can moan and groan about it—or you can pick up and go.'"

Pick up and go. But truly, the only place Natalie wanted to go was home. She pulled out her iPod and curled up to listen to music.

They were about halfway into the ride, just outside Frederick, with the deaf students aboard, when Serena tapped her on the shoulder and asked if she could sit beside her.

"Sure," Natalie said. She sat up and lifted the heavy Brailler she was taking home for the holiday break and set it on the floor to make room.

"How's it going?" Serena asked.

Natalie shrugged. "Okay, I guess."

"I'm glad you stayed so you could come to my birthday party," Serena said.

"Sure. It was fun. Good ice cream."

"Yeah." She sighed. "So! Do you want me to teach you how to say 'asshole' in sign language?"

"What?! Is that what you sign with the deaf kids? You're cussing with them?"

"Hey, they're the ones who taught me!"

"*Serena!* . . . No. I don't want to know how to swear in sign language."

They rode in silence for a ways, until Serena said in a serious voice, "I just want you to know that I know how you feel."

"Thanks," Natalie said. "I appreciate it."

"No. Like I mean that I *really* know how you feel," Serena went on. "Like when I lost my right eye I was devastated. Ms. Kravitz says I'm still angry about it and that's why I'm always saying mean things to people. I don't know. Maybe she's right. Maybe I *am* still angry."

Natalie was frowning as she turned toward Serena. "I thought your right eye was your good eye."

"No. My right eye's gone."

"The sight, you mean."

"No. The whole eye. It's gone. *Enucleated,* if you've never heard the term."

"But—"

"Hold out your hand."

"What for?"

"Hold out your hand," Serena repeated.

Natalie opened her hand slowly, unsure of Serena's intentions.

Serena put something small in her palm and closed Natalie's fingers around it. "Can you feel it?"

"What is it? A stone?"

Serena leaned in to whisper, "It's my *eye* dummy. My glass eye!"

Startled, Natalie sucked in her breath and put her other hand on her chest.

"It's okay. It's not going to bite you!"

"I'm not afraid."

"What, then? You're grossed out?"

"No!" Natalie insisted. "It's just that I've never—*held* anyone's eye before."

"Go ahead. Feel it."

Delicately, Natalie touched it with her index finger. It was very smooth, rounded on one side, flat on the other, about the size of a peach stone—and about the same size as her HOPE stone.

"That's the one good brown eye you thought I had. My real eye, the one I actually see some out of—well, it's not so great, and I'm sure I'll lose that one, too."

"Gosh," Natalie sympathized.

"Yeah. Did I ever tell you why?"

Natalie shook her head. "No."

"Okay. You ready for this one? Toxoplasmosis. Courtesy of my mother when she was pregnant with me. It's a disease you get from cats, like from their litter, *or* from uncooked meat. My mother doesn't even like cats, so she says it was probably an undercooked burger or something. Who knows? So anyway, bad luck is the bottom line. That's why I get depressed. And that's why I'm at the school in Baltimore. So they can be sure I take my meds, and keep an eye out—ha! so to speak!— that I don't cut myself, too. I was a big-time cutter back in my public school. But you would be, too, if you had to deal with those kids."

"Serena. The whole strap of your pocketbook has safety pins on it!"

"I know! They're there just in case. You'd think somebody would say something, wouldn't you? But honestly, I don't think a single person has ever noticed. Anyway, I'm over it now. The cutting stuff. That was juvenile crap anyway. You know? My little cry for attention."

"Why are you telling me this?"

There was a slight pause before Serena replied. "Because I want you to know that you're not alone, that I truly understand how you must feel right now. And I want you to know that I'm sorry if I've ever said anything that offends you."

Natalie sighed. "I appreciate it," she said, with a mere trace of a smile. "Especially since I don't think I've ever heard you apologize for anything."

"Yeah, well, you know what they say: seeing is believing. So I guess you'll never know for sure. You'll just have to trust me. I am definitely apologizing."

Natalie's smile became full. "Thanks, Serena," she said. "And oh, here's your eye back."

MIXED BLESSINGS

Cold weather always came early to Garrett County, but there was one last farmers market on the Saturday before Thanksgiving. Baskets of apples, jugs of cider, and a colorful array of squash and pumpkins were displayed on hay bales. The Amish brought eggs and fresh, warm baked goods. Natalie's mother had already scooped up two of their pies, as well as a few cream-filled pumpkin gobs for Uncle Jack. The flea market was open, too, with everything from Beanie Babies and hand-painted saws to secondhand dishes and old irons for door stoppers. Or so Natalie's mother told her.

Natalie, wearing jeans and a heavy sweater, moved her cane over the rough, uneven ground outside, staying close to her mother's side. She was self-conscious using the cane in public, but she knew it was crucial now.

"A few craftspeople are here. They have hand-knit baby clothing and blankets. And—oh, gosh—who in the world is going to buy a box of old LP records?" Her mother kept up a running commentary that was becoming a little too loud and embarrassing, Natalie thought. And why did she have to sound so upbeat? Was she getting some enjoyment out of this? But even as she thought it, Natalie knew she was just taking her anger out on her mother again.

"Nat, the honey lady is here. She's waving us over."

Natalie wondered if the honey lady would say anything about the cane, but she didn't. She just rambled on in her Southern accent about what a nice day it was and how they simply had to sample her new goldenrod honey. "Y'all have to try it. I'm gonna insist. Here, I've got some little crackers. There you go." Talking as if nothing was different. But everything was different. So what was she thinking? She must have been thinking *something*. Natalie wanted to see her face and her expression and the way she moved her hands. You could tell so much from the way people moved their hands. But nothing. A cracker with honey sat in Natalie's mouth.

Back at their van, cheese sales were brisk. Natalie was busy filling bags and inserting flyers all morning. Lots of people had questions about the cheese, and different voices filled the air. But along about noon, a familiar one struck a chord. "Natalie. It's Jake. Jake Handelman."

Turning toward the voice, Natalie smiled. "Hi!" With her foot, she pushed the folded cane under her chair.

"How are you doing?"

"Okay, Jake. How are you?" It was weird running into him again at the market. Natalie wondered if it was possible that he actually came looking for her.

"Things are great," he said with his usual enthusiasm. "I'm going to the student council conference in Omaha next month."

"Congratulations!" Natalie told him.

"Yeah. I'm excited, even if it is just Nebraska. But heck, I've never been anywhere west of Ohio."

"No, I haven't either," Natalie said. "It should be fun."

Jake's voice became more subdued. "I wish you were going, too, though," he said. "We miss you on the council, Nat. We miss you at school."

Natalie's throat got tight. She wanted to tell Jake that maybe she'd be back next year—by senior year for sure—but couldn't seem to get the words out. And she wondered if he knew she was blind now. Could he tell? Natalie would have given anything to have been able to see his face. Was he looking at her? Feeling sad? Indifferent? What?

"Hey, so anyway, we love your cheese. My mom, she loves that new spread with the ginger in it."

Natalie nodded and smiled. "My mom invented it. I like it, too. My dad said a major grocery chain is picking it up for the holidays."

"Cool!"

Another silent pause. Should she tell him she was blind? But maybe he was in a rush to go. Was he? Or did he want to stay and talk? Was there a customer waiting? How was she ever going to know these things?

"Well, anyway, have a great Thanksgiving, Nat."

"Yeah! You too," she replied, not really wanting him to leave.

Then, two days later, in late afternoon, Meredith showed up. Natalie hadn't talked to her for nearly three weeks.

"She's coming up the front walk now, Nat. Shall I have her come in?" Natalie's mother asked. "She must really want to see you, coming over in all this snow. There must be three inches already."

Natalie sat on the living-room couch and pushed the mute button on the television's remote control. "Does she *know*?"

A slight pause. "Yes," her mother said. "I saw Meredith's mother at the post office a couple days ago."

Suddenly angry, Natalie sat up. "What? Did you ask her to bring Meredith over or something?"

"No! No, I didn't," her mother insisted.

There was a knock at the door.

Natalie sighed. An exasperated sigh.

Her mother was waiting.

"Yeah, sure," Natalie finally said. "Go ahead and let her in."

Natalie turned the television off. As the heavy front door was opened, cold air rushed into the room, and Natalie heard her mother and Meredith greet each other. There was the stomping of boots and the unzipping of a coat. Natalie pictured Meredith in her burgundy parka—with a scarf. She always had a scarf knotted around her neck. Footsteps. Natalie could smell the snow that must have clung to Meredith's long hair. The sleeves of her parka brushed against her sides and made a rustling sound as she came closer. Natalie stood, but wasn't sure if Meredith was right in front of her or taking a seat.

"I am so sorry, Nat," Meredith said. When she spoke, Natalie could tell she was to her right, very close. Meredith sniffed and her voice had a nasal timbre to it, as if she'd been crying. "I had no idea you were actually going to lose all your sight."

"Yeah. Well, I guess I never wanted to believe it myself."

"And here I am, the world's worst friend. . . . I'm sure you hate me."

"No." Natalie took a breath. "I don't hate you, Meredith. Actually, I understand. Richie's like the first real boyfriend you've had."

An awkward, quiet moment followed.

Natalie's mother, who must have been listening, called into the room: "Nat, be sure to tell Meredith the exciting news!"

Annoyed that her mother was eavesdropping, Natalie said, "Mom!"

"What?" Meredith touched Natalie's wrist. "What's the news?"

And Natalie couldn't help but grin. "Nuisance is pregnant. She's due at Christmastime."

"No way!" Meredith exclaimed. "Nat, that's exciting!" She reached out then to touch one of Natalie's hands. "Come on. Can we be friends?"

Natalie nodded, and the old friends hugged for a long moment.

A trip to the mall was not Natalie's idea of a fun thing to do, but Meredith had begged her. "Come on. We *always* go shopping the day before Thanksgiving when we don't have school. My mom said she'd drive us over to LaVale and drop us off. We can have lunch with Coralee and Suzanne, and then you and I can shop and talk and catch up. *Please*. It'll be fun."

"I'm not sure, Meres. I can't see anything."

"But I can describe stuff to you, and if you bring your Christmas list we could get a little of it done."

Nervous, Natalie licked her lips and pressed them together, thinking. "The other thing is that I'm not sure I can use my cane very well. I wouldn't want to run into someone."

"Oh." Meredith sounded disappointed.

"I mean, I guess we could do sighted guide."

"What's that?" Meredith asked.

"Where I just hold your elbow and let you lead."

"Yeah! Let's do that! It'll be fine. Just show me what to do."

So at the mall Natalie carried her cane in a tote bag (just in case) and reminded Meredith to take it slow. "I'm going to tuck my right hand in around your elbow and walk maybe a half step behind.

But you just walk normal—and let me know if something big comes up—like stairs!"

Meredith laughed. "Okay. I can handle that."

The mall was packed. "I'm going to stay toward the edge," Meredith said. "Fewer people."

"Sounds good," Natalie told her.

They hit all their favorite stores first: American Eagle, Aéropostale, Claire's. "Look at these earrings," Meredith said, putting a pair of enormous hoops in Natalie's hand. "Can you tell how big they are? They're so big, they're gross."

"Oh, these sweaters are beautiful!" Meredith gushed a few minutes later. She took Natalie's hand and guided it to the display. "Isn't it soft?"

Natalie nodded. "Very soft."

"Half off! And they're turtleneck, Nat. You love turtlenecks. They come in green, a deep red like wine, and black. Do you want to try one on?"

The thought of using a dressing room, and then not being able to see herself, was too much for Natalie. "No thanks," she said. "Maybe later."

At noon, they met Coralee and Suzanne at Chick-fil-A for lunch. Each of the girls gave Natalie a hug.

"Sorry about your sight," Coralee said.

"Yeah, that's a real bummer," Suzanne added.

Natalie didn't think either of the girls sounded overly sincere. But what did she expect? Would she rather hear them choking back sobs? No. No way. She had to give them some credit: at least they acknowledged her blindness instead of ignoring it. The four girls ordered their meals and sat down at a small table together.

"What's it like?" Suzanne asked. "I mean, can you see like light versus dark?

"No." Natalie shook her head. "Nothing."

"I heard that when people lose their sight, their sense of hearing gets better," Coralee said. "Is that true?"

"No, my hearing is the same. It's hasn't changed," Natalie said. "It's just that I'm more tuned into it. I use it more. It becomes more important."

"Wow. I think if I ever lost my sight, I'd get one of those dogs," Suzanne said. "Why don't you get a Seeing Eye dog? *I* would."

Natalie smiled at her ignorance. "They're called guide dogs. And, well, for starters, you can't just *get a dog*. You have to be a certain age, and you need to learn how to use the cane first, because what if the dog gets sick? What if you need to go somewhere and the dog is not allowed? You need to be able to get around without a dog, too."

Suzanne was quiet. Natalie hoped she hadn't been too preachy.

Natalie felt a slender thread of tension wending its way through the group. Was it because of her blindness? She didn't want to ruin the meal. But she didn't want to turn it into a big Q and A about being blind either, so she tried to reverse the conversation.

"How about you guys? How's school? Meredith—how are things with Richard? I mean, Richie?" she asked brightly, before dipping a chicken strip in barbecue sauce and taking a bite.

"Good! He went to Richmond with his family to have Thanksgiving with his grandparents. They're looking at a college down there, too."

"I forgot he's a senior," Natalie said. "How did you meet him anyway?"

"At a party," she said.

Suzanne giggled. "It was a blackout party."

"Yeah. That was so weird, wasn't it?" Coralee added. "You couldn't *see* anybody! I was talking to this boy. I thought he was really nice and he turned out to be this really ugly creep!"

The two girls laughed, but Natalie felt the blood drain from her face.

Meredith made a noise, and both girls instantly shut up.

"Ew. Sorry," Coralee mumbled.

"Yeah. We didn't mean anything," Suzanne said.

Natalie tilted her face down. She stopped chewing, and the food made a lump in her mouth. *How could they?* She swallowed and wiped her hands on a napkin. *So incredibly insensitive.* Was it time to go? She wanted to go. Just *go*.

"How much do I owe you anyway?" she asked Meredith, trying to keep the emotion out of her voice. She reached for her wallet. Her mother had put two ten-dollar bills in it.

"You don't owe me anything," Meredith said, pulling Natalie's hand away from her pocketbook. "My treat today."

Coralee and Suzanne remained silent, and the four of them finished quickly.

"That was stupid of them. I am so sorry," Meredith apologized, her voice hushed, as they walked back down the corridor of the mall. Suzanne and Coralee had gone in the other direction. "They're really assholes sometimes, you know it?"

Natalie's arm brushed against what she guessed was a potted plant. "Yeah. I do know it," she agreed, beaming at Meredith's comment. She'd known it for a long time.

All at once, a warm feeling washed her face, and it struck Natalie that they must be in the mall's center court, under the skylight.

They walked in and out of Payless, where Meredith was on the lookout for a new pair of black shoes, then drifted in front of Bath & Body Works for a free body lotion sample. "Ummm. It's new: Rainkissed Leaves. Nice," Meredith murmured. She held a tube up to Natalie's nose, then put a dab on the back of Natalie's hand so she could rub it in and try it. Resuming sighted guide, they left the store and walked down the corridor.

Suddenly, a boy's voice behind them called out: "Hey there, you two lovers!"

Meredith stiffened. Her head swung around and then back. Natalie could feel the motions.

"Is he talking to *us*?" Meredith asked angrily.

"You two lesbos holding hands!" The boy's voice came closer.

Natalie's mind reeled: did they think they were lesbians because she was holding Meredith's elbow for guidance?

"Can I have a smooch, too?" He snuck up behind them, making obscene little kissing noises.

"Beat it!" Meredith spit out. She pulled away with a jerk and it made Natalie tighten her grip.

"Come on, let's get out of here," Meredith said, quickening her step.

Natalie was nervous walking so fast, but Meredith did not slow down until they were clear outside the mall.

"Here's a bench, Nat. Sit down," she said.

Natalie felt behind her and sat, letting go of Meredith's arm.

"Idiots!" Meredith muttered. She paced in front of the bench, and Natalie wondered if she was still watching for the boys.

"I'm sorry, Meres," Natalie said as she set her tote bag on her lap. She was not only embarrassed and angry, but sorry that Meredith was upset. "Did you know those boys?"

"No! Never seen them before in my life! What a couple of jerks!"

"Look, I'll get my cane out," Natalie offered, pulling it from her tote bag. "I'll use that instead."

But Meredith was firm. "Let's just call my mom, okay?"

THE DYNAMICS OF FIGHTING

"Is fighting for you?" a male voice on the tape began. "You may find yourself in a situation in which someone won't take no for an answer."

On the long bus ride back to school there was a lot to think about, and Natalie had to restart the recording several times. She still hadn't gotten over the incident in the mall with Meredith. It blew her away that those boys thought they were lesbians.

Reluctantly, Natalie returned to her homework and put on her earphones so she could listen to a tape of Chapter Five in the self-defense book.

"You learned how awareness, intuition, and setting boundaries are your first lines of defense in avoiding an attack," the tape continued. "Now we'll discuss fighting back as part of your personal safety plan.

"Are you committed to fighting back if you are attacked?" the tape asked. "Are you willing to risk being seriously injured in order to survive?"

Natalie had never asked herself those questions before. She wasn't sure how to answer.

Then the tape issued this warning: "Don't ever believe a criminal, whether armed or not, who says, 'If you stay quiet, do what I say, and come with me, I won't hurt you.' Police statistics reveal that in situations in which an armed assailant convinces his victim to get into a car, the victim's chance of survival is a mere two percent. . . ."

Natalie turned off the CD player and tried to mentally recap the points made. *Women who have fought attackers—and won— had several things in common. They were committed to disabling their attacker. They were prepared to be hurt. They acted as quickly as possible. They did not allow themselves to be taken to a second crime scene.*

"Facing Panic" was next. And panic was followed by yelling— how important it was to keep yelling during an attack, because it draws attention and keeps you breathing. Natalie clicked off the player again. It was scary to imagine a situation where she would face panic and have to yell her head off. The whole discussion was beginning to make her nervous. She thought of Miss Karen, her Braille instructor, who took two different buses to get to work every day—and then walked the last mile to school. It would be so easy for someone to take advantage of her. On the other hand, what were her options? Have a friend or relative take her everywhere? What if no one was available? The school receptionist sometimes waited two hours for the Paratransit van to show up. It was inexpensive and safe, she had once told Natalie. But who wanted to spend half their life waiting around?

Being blind, it seemed, was a no-win situation.

As if things weren't bad enough, when Natalie arrived back at school, she walked into her room to find Bree already there, softly crying.

"What's wrong?" Natalie asked as she settled her duffel on the bed.

When Bree didn't respond, Natalie approached Bree's bed, where she thought Bree was sitting, then made sure with her hand that there was an open space to sit down beside her. She put a hand on Bree's back. "What happened?"

"It's Kirk." Bree sniffed. "My boyfriend. He's seeing someone else. I found out when I was home. He thinks because I'm blind now that I can't see what's going on! Well, I may not have a lot of friends, but I do have people looking out for me!

"That's not the only thing, Nat. When I got home, when I got out of Aunt Stina's car, I used my cane to get in the house, and he was sitting there on the stoop waiting for me. He says, 'What's that?' And I tell him, 'It's my cane.' And he says to me, 'Well, you ain't takin' *that* anywhere with *me*!'"

The two girls were silent for a moment.

"Bree, anyone who says that must not care very much for you. Not really. Because if they did, they would understand that you need that cane. In the long run, this is best. You don't want to have to depend on him."

"You're right," Bree declared, surprising Natalie. "You know, I've been thinking about it. *A lot.* I want to learn everything, the way you are, so I don't have to depend on a lowlife like him anymore. I'm serious. I told my aunt I was going to change and really try."

"Then we'll learn it together, Bree. We'll learn what we have to together, okay?"

Another sniff. "Yeah. And Kirk will be sorry."

"From now on, we move forward." Natalie surprised herself at what a good pep talk she could deliver. Amazing what a phony she was! Because hadn't she kicked her own cane under the chair when Jake showed up at the farmers' market?

"From now on, Nat," Bree repeated.

A soft "okay" was all that Natalie could manage.

The next morning it was pouring rain, but neither Natalie nor Bree realized it until they were at the front door. The dorm counselor sent them back to their room for raincoats and told them to check the radio for weather before they got dressed in the morning.

"And tell Serena to hurry up or we're leaving without her!" the counselor called after them.

Natalie and Bree returned for rain slickers and umbrellas and, on their way back, Natalie turned toward Serena's room and called in, "Hurry up! Or we're leaving without you!"

"I just need to find my umbrella!" Serena called back.

Natalie stopped, mesmerized, and took several slow steps inside the door of Serena's room.

Serena stopped rifling through her closet. "I told you, I'll be right—Nat, what's up? What's wrong? Why are you looking like that?"

Natalie pointed to Serena's bureau. "I think I can see your little plug-in Christmas tree. The one you brought from home. It's all lit up."

"Oh, my gosh, Nat. You can *see* it?"

Natalie walked toward it, holding out her hand until she had touched the tiny branches.

"Whoa. That's like incredible," Serena said. She unplugged the tree. The lights went out and Natalie's hand fell away.

"Now they're gone," Natalie said.

Serena plugged it back in.

"Now they're on!"

"Nat!" Serena exclaimed.

Natalie smiled with excitement. "What do you think this means?"

"I don't know. But we'd better get going, 'cause I do know what it means if that woman has to come and get us. Come on."

On the walk to breakfast, everything was back to normal—that is, no sight, just the gray screen. But what did it mean, seeing those lights? That her sight was returning? There was some recovery? As soon as she could, she would call her mother so she could phone Dr. Rose and ask him.

In American government class, Natalie turned in the paper she had written over break. She had typed the entire assignment on her Brailler, even using the small wooden "eraser" to smooth out letters incorrectly punched. It had taken hours to finish the paper, in which she had concluded that she was in favor of changing the feel of currency. "Blind people should not have to depend on the kindness of strangers," she wrote, "to tell them what money they have in their hands—especially if it's money they earned."

At lunch, everyone shared stories of their vacations at home. Arnab couldn't stop talking about all the wonderful, spicy Indian food he'd eaten. Bree complained about a killer headache she'd had, but didn't mention Kirk. And JJ had greeted a new baby half sister. Natalie wanted to tell everyone about seeing the Christmas lights in Serena's room, but she was afraid to jinx it. Every chance she had, however, she reached into her pocket to rub the pink stone. The biggest news at lunch came from the whispered rumors that Eve and Sheldon were "going out" now, and that they had even visited each other over the break.

"Don't you think that's a little shocking?" Murph said to Natalie and Serena as they left the lunch table together. "I mean, she's white and he's black."

Serena stopped in her tracks. "What? Are you a racist now? In addition to being a moron? Like the color of someone's skin really matters—especially to two people who can't even see each other!"

Natalie cringed at the "moron" part, but otherwise was glad this time for Serena's quick tongue.

"It makes no difference if you're weak or strong! Or if you have a black belt in karate! Self-defense is a mindset!" Mr. Lee told the girls eagerly assembled for gym class.

He had them pair up and stand ten to fifteen feet apart. "If you're attacked," he said, "you need to be close to your attacker to fight back."

A drill followed: one girl remained standing while the other talked—and walked—toward her partner. "Your job," he told the standing girl, "is to reach out when you think your partner is in striking distance and touch the crook of her neck. The spot where your shoulder and neck meet is called the Universal Reference Point. The URP. This is important!"

After a few rounds, Natalie was able to tell when she was close enough to Bree to reach out and touch the URP on her neck.

"Listen to your attacker!" Mr. Lee advised them while they practiced. "Hearing your attacker speak, or yell, gives you valuable clues as to where his head is located—and therefore where you should aim! Grab the URP with your *nonstriking* hand! This leaves the other hand free to strike back."

The girls rested for a moment and Mr. Lee lowered his voice.

"You should know that the human body has many weapons of its own. You can use your hands, for example, to make a fist. The hard knuckle area is called the ridge. Feel how hard those knuckles are. Now open your hand. The area between your pinkie finger—that's right, your little finger—and the wrist is called the blade." From the sound of it, Natalie imagined he was making a hacking motion and hitting the palm of one hand with the blade of the other.

"You also have the heel of your palm," he added, making a different kind of hard, slapping sound.

"You girls have fingers that can be used to poke—grab—rip—gouge—and squeeze!

"Fingernails! Do you girls have good fingernails?" he continued, his voice growing louder. "They may be polished and pretty, but those fingernails are good for scratching! Also to stab, poke—and slit!"

Natalie's stomach knotted up. Using her fingers to slit? Slit *what*?

"Elbows!" Mr. Lee called out. "Elbows make good hammers! Feet can kick. Feet can push away, stomp—and scrape!

"Knees!" he shouted. "Knees can be used to ram into an attacker's body. Is the attacker behind you? Use the back of your head to slam into his face!"

Yikes. Smash her head into someone?

"Teeth!" Mr. Lee called out. "Use those teeth to bite!"

Mr. Lee then recited a morbid list of body parts that were prime targets: eyes, nose, throat, solar plexus (the soft spot in your chest), ribs, knees, and shins. "Shins are a nerve sandwich," he pointed out. "So kick that attacker's shin! Scrape it with the side of your foot!

"And remember! There are no rules when it comes to defending your life. Most men—trust Mr. Lee—don't want to get kicked in the groin. Testicles are major nerve centers between a man's legs."

Even though she couldn't see, Natalie's eyes opened wide. Was Mr. Lee telling them to kick a man between the legs?

Kicking a man in the groin was not the only thing Mr. Lee encouraged. He also advised them to "grab those testicles. It causes even greater pain if you rotate that grip."

Natalie dropped her head, embarrassed. She wanted to tune out, but Mr. Lee's voice was so compelling she couldn't.

"All right. Girls, stand up!" he ordered them. "Let's practice kicking, grabbing, and punching an imaginary attacker.

"Make a fist!" Mr. Lee hollered. "Send that punch flying! Rotate those hips for a complete follow-through!"

Natalie went through the motions, but could she ever fight like this? She didn't think so. It was like something in a movie, she thought, not something you'd actually *do* to anyone.

Unless, of course, your life was on the line. But even then, could she really *do* these things?

Halfheartedly she practiced; there was no way for her to know then that the biggest test of those skills was just around the corner.

CROSSING OVER

What did he say, Mom?" Natalie whispered urgently because no one was supposed to make phone calls from their rooms in the morning.

"Dr. Rose said not to get your hopes up," her mother said. When she sighed, Natalie braced herself. "Seeing the Christmas lights is not unusual. There may be a tiny bit of vision left to one side, a 'temporal island,' he called it."

Natalie held the phone to her ear and felt her heart drop down into the soles of her feet.

"Nat, are you there?"

"Yes," she finally replied. "So none of my vision is coming back?"

"Dr. Rose said that little bit may come and go. But it doesn't mean anything, Nat."

It doesn't mean anything. Unbelievable. How could it not *mean* something?!

Natalie felt as though her emotions were on a roller coaster. Chugging uphill one day, then plunging downhill the next. *A temporal island.* Another disappointment. You'd think she'd be used to it by now.

"Are you ready?" Miss Audra asked.

A simple enough question. Natalie shrugged, but the answer was no, actually. She wasn't ready. She would never be ready. She was just going through the motions.

"Natalie, come on. This is important. This is your test. You're basically walking by yourself to the Forestville Shopping Center. I'll be with you, but I'm not supposed to say much."

"I understand," Natalie responded. By then, they'd done the entire walk several times. Natalie wasn't afraid, nor excited. She just felt—*flat* about it. She couldn't even fake enthusiasm. After finding out the little lights didn't mean anything, she hadn't been able to rebound. All the way to the traffic light on Dunbar Avenue, Natalie tried to listen carefully as she swept her cane, moving forward. At the traffic light, however, after she pressed the button for the traffic light and waited at the curb, the nonchalance evaporated.

She listened as traffic directly in front of her stopped. She listened as traffic to her right moved. This was her opportunity to cross. Extending her cane, she tapped three times to signal her intention, but her feet suddenly filled with lead and her wrist froze.

Miss Audra said nothing.

Natalie took another breath, then cracked through her fear to move her wrist. She tapped her cane again. *Come on, you've done this before. It's not that hard. Just do it and get it over with.* But the sound of her own breathing filled her head and her heart thumped rapidly, high in her chest.

All at once, traffic in front of her was moving again, while traffic to the right had stopped. She had lost her opportunity.

Her shoulders sagged. She would have to wait for another cycle. Embarrassed, she pressed the button on the traffic light again and stood stiffly, biting her bottom lip.

A few minutes passed. Miss Audra didn't speak. When traffic in front of Natalie again stopped, and it was time to go, Natalie extended her cane into the road and tapped three times. She took a deep breath and forced one foot off the curb, then pulled the other cinder-block foot behind it. Miss Audra would tell her if a car was coming, right? Another step. She wouldn't let Natalie kill herself. No way. She'd get fired. One more step and then she was moving, *really moving*, her cane sweeping quickly, until she reached the other side.

"Good!" Miss Audra said.

Relief poured out of Natalie and her heart thumped madly.

Over the next half mile, Natalie knew there would be three smaller streets to cross, but no big intersections with traffic lights. Then, just before the entrance to the shopping center, a large utility box would be on the right.

A dog barked, startling Natalie, and she jumped, bumping into Miss Audra. She hadn't run into any dogs before.

"It's okay," Miss Audra assured her, putting a hand on Natalie's arm. "He's fenced in. But remember, don't act afraid. It would only excite a dog more. Now, lots of houses coming up on your left, remember? Most have fenced yards and short sidewalks leading up to their steps."

Natalie appreciated the reminder and continued until the sound of a plastic-wheeled tricycle thundering toward them ground their progress to a halt. She stepped to one side and held her cane in front of her.

"Megan!" An older woman's voice. "Stop! You're scaring those people!"

The noisy tricycle stopped. "What's wrong with her?" a small voice asked. "Why does she have that stick, Mommy?"

"Shhhhhh!" the mother said, urging the child on.

"It's all right," Miss Audra whispered. "Pretty soon, that big cemetery comes up, remember? It'll be quieter there."

Natalie had tried to make a mental map of the streets, the houses, the cemetery, and the shopping center and was trying to visualize where she was when her cane caught on something that tripped her. Natalie caught herself before falling and kneeled, gently examining the item in her way. It felt like an empty pizza box. She moved it off the sidewalk and continued, but a few steps later, her cane jammed into a large crack and pushed the cane's grip into her stomach.

"Argh!" Natalie exclaimed. "That hurt!"

It made her a little angry that Miss Audra didn't sympathize.

Suddenly, the *whap* against metal. That would be the utility box. The shopping center was just ahead, on the left.

"All right," said Miss Audra, putting a hand on Natalie's shoulder. "You have arrived. Remember, the Super Fresh is on your left. People will be pushing carts and loading groceries into cars parked along the right-hand side. Remember to go slowly and be careful. There are a lot of elderly people, some of them with walkers, who can't move quickly."

Beyond the supermarket, Natalie had memorized the series of stores: first the liquor store, then the nail salon and the Raven's Nest Bar, followed by the Rite Aid pharmacy, the Hallmark store, and finally, the Parthenon, the Greek restaurant, where they were meeting Arnab and his cane instructor, Mr. Greg, for dinner.

The rest of the walk was easy, and when the air suddenly filled with the smell of bread and garlic, Natalie knew they had arrived. It never felt so good to sit down. A few minutes later, Arnab and Mr.

Greg joined them. Introductions were made—Natalie didn't know Mr. Greg—and Arnab didn't know Miss Audra. Arnab took a seat beside Natalie, then reached over, under the table, to touch her arm and squeeze her hand. "Hi," he said softly.

"Hi," she replied. She felt a bit uneasy with him touching her that way. Was it because weeks ago she had allowed him to touch her face? Did that mean something more to him than it did to her? Because, while it made Natalie feel wanted—and she did enjoy the attention—she didn't think of Arnab as her boyfriend now. Did he interpret things differently? Natalie rubbed her hands on her jeans nervously. These weren't bad feelings, just kind of mixed-up feelings.

Suddenly, the waiter was there, taking drink orders and suggesting they try the new barbecue chicken pizza, which sounded good to all of them. Then, since Arnab had just completed the same walk as Natalie, there was a lot of comparing to do: the dog that barked, the hair-raising crossing at the traffic light, the crowds near the supermarket.

"And did you hit that crack in the sidewalk?" Arnab asked.

"I hit that crack every time!" Natalie exclaimed.

"Such a pain!" Arnab laughed.

"Well, here's to an excellent walk," Miss Audra said. "To Arnab and Natalie. I'm holding my glass for a toast."

"Two jobs well done!" Mr. Greg chimed in.

No. It wasn't a job well done, and Natalie knew it. She about had heart failure crossing that big intersection. Maybe Arnab deserved this pass, but she sure didn't. She would never use it. She didn't even want it! Nevertheless, Natalie lifted her water glass, and somehow they all managed to clink their glasses together in a toast.

"I mean it, Natalie, you can do anything you set your mind to doing," Miss Audra went on. "It's all about self-confidence."

"Absolutely," Mr. Greg agreed.

"About the only thing you won't be able to do in your life is drive a car and fly an airplane," Miss Audra added. "Oh—and you probably can't be a surgeon."

Natalie grinned and scrunched up her nose. "That's okay," she said. "I never much liked the idea of cutting into people."

Mr. Greg laughed. "Another toast!" he said. "Today, the Forestville Shopping Center, tomorrow Thailand—or Paris—or Venice! Actually, I would not recommend Venice because of the water."

"You have been there?" Arnab asked.

"Yes. Twice, in fact. Once with a friend and once on my own."

"On your own? You are serious, Mr. Greg? You went to Venice on your own, even though you are blind?" Arnab was incredulous.

"Yes!" he replied.

"Mr. Greg has traveled all over the world," Miss Audra noted. "He just got back from Scotland."

"But why?" Natalie asked. "Why travel if you can't *see* anything?"

"Good question. I have been asked this many times. And I always remind people that there are many ways to measure beauty other than sight. For example, I can *smell* the ocean, I can *feel* the energy of the wind."

"But Scotland, Mr. Greg?" Arnab asked.

"Oh, Scotland. Well! The sound of the bagpipes, for one thing. And the accent. There was the hustle and bustle in the pubs, the laughter and the clinking of glasses. And the bumpy cobblestoned streets everywhere, and the cold feel of those weathered stone walls and buildings. And oh, yes, the feel of a cold pint in my hand, and the warm wool tartan around my neck, and the peppery taste of haggis. These are not things that require sight."

Natalie was astonished at the details he brought to life.

"You should be a writer," Arnab said.

"There is a documentary called *Blindsight* that I want you to hear sometime," Miss Audra said. "It's about a mountain climber named Erik Weihenmayer who is blind. The first blind person to climb Mount Everest, in fact. But *Blindsight* is not about that adventure. It is a documentary about how he leads six blind Tibetan teenagers up a twenty-three-thousand-foot mountain."

Just as Natalie was trying to absorb that incredible idea, the pizza arrived. It smelled wonderful. Miss Audra served them each a piece and handed out napkins. "It's really hot," she said. "Be careful."

They enjoyed the pizza. When it was time to pay, Natalie was surprised to hear Arnab offer to take the bill.

"But it was going to be my treat," Miss Audra said.

"No, no. Mine, *please*, Miss Audra. Please let me pay. It is a small thank you for what you and Mr. Greg are doing."

"Okay," Miss Audra agreed. "How nice. Well, let's see. It came to twenty-three dollars and fifteen cents with all the drinks."

"Let me get my wallet out," Arnab said.

Natalie wondered how he was going to do this. Would he just hand over his wallet to Miss Audra and ask her to take what was needed?

"Here is a twenty," he said. "And here—three ones. Okay, one dime. Yes, yes. And a nickel. Yes, and a five-dollar bill for the tip."

"Excellent," Miss Audra said. "Although that's a pretty hefty tip."

"It is okay," Arnab said. "It was good service."

"Great job," Mr. Greg commented.

After the waiter took the money and thanked them, Natalie leaned over to Arnab. "Okay," she said. "So you have a system. How did you know your twenty from your ones?"

"Oh! Mr. Greg taught me this," Arnab said. "It's not hard. A bill simply folded in half is a one-dollar bill." He pushed a folded bill into her hands. "Folded in half a second time means it is a five-dollar bill. Folded in half yet again, into a small square, it means a ten. A twenty-dollar bill—it is folded in half lengthwise. The long way. And if you are lucky enough to have a fifty, then it's folded in a triangle."

"What about the change?" Natalie asked.

"Easy," Arnab told her. "Quarters have ridges. A dime is a small quarter. Pennies and nickels have smooth edges. The penny is smaller than the nickel."

So there *was* a system, Natalie realized.

It was time to go. Both Natalie and Arnab reached beneath their chairs for their folded canes. Natalie pulled on her jacket.

Back at school, Miss Audra gave Natalie a hug, but Natalie's arms hung limp at her side. She had gotten through the evening but didn't exactly feel encouraged by it. The truth was that she wished she was home, with her parents, where she knew her way around the house and wouldn't have to deal with money, or put her life on the line crossing a busy intersection.

"What's wrong?" Miss Audra asked. "You should be proud of what you accomplished today."

"That's just it, Miss Audra. I don't feel proud. Because I won't ever be able to do all these things on my own."

"Look, no one expects you to climb a mountain in Tibet or visit Scotland next week on your own."

"It's not just that, though. It's the little, everyday stuff. Like Miss Karen taking that bus to work. And Arnab paying for dinner. I can't *imagine* myself ever doing those things. It's not *in* me to do that!"

"It *is* in you. But it takes practice. It takes self-confidence," Miss Audra insisted. "You can do it if you want to. You know, I always tell my students at some point that when they leave here, they will need to make a huge decision. And that decision is how they are going to live their lives.

"Think about this, Natalie: Will you utilize the skills you are learning here to go out and embrace the world?" Miss Audra paused. "Or will you go home to Mom and Dad and hide out, living scared?"

WHY NOT?

It was difficult to keep a straight face the next day when a rubber penis was passed around in health class. Miss La Verne had warned sternly against "laughter or inappropriate comments." But even Natalie had to slap a hand over her mouth when Serena squealed as the rubber penis ejaculated water in her hands.

Natalie had wondered if this was really necessary (it seemed so startling at first, so *bizarre*), but then she thought of Eve and some of the others who had been blind from birth. They'd never seen those pictures and diagrams in the middle-school health ed books.

The crinkly sound of a foil package being torn open next drew the girls' attention. "This is called a condom," Miss La Verne told them, going on to describe how, and why, it was used. Natalie thought to herself that whatever job she had in the future, it would *not* be as health instructor at a school for the blind.

"It's like a water balloon," Serena joked when it was her turn to examine the condom.

"Serena, do you need to leave the class?" Miss La Verne asked.

"No way!" Serena replied. "I'm sorry, Miss La Verne. I'll be good. I promise."

Natalie and Bree were still chuckling about it that night as they sat on their beds. Bree had just taught Natalie how to knit, and Natalie was working on a blue scarf, one slow stitch at a time, each of which had to be counted. She planned to give her mother the scarf for Christmas.

"Serena is something else, you know it?" Natalie said. "Whatever you may think of her, though, she does have a beautiful voice. I heard her sing today."

"You did?"

"Yes. She tried to get me to join chorus with her."

"She asked me, too!" Bree noted.

"Maybe we should do it. Why not?"

Bree's voice grew serious. "I need to apologize to her. To all of them for what I said that first day. I can't believe I called them a bunch of freaks."

"Yeah, but I think they understand, Bree."

"Still."

"Someday, maybe, when you feel the time is right," Natalie said. She slipped the yarn around her metal knitting needle and, with a soft scraping sound, carefully pulled the next stitch through.

Bree was quiet. Again, without being able to see a person's face, it was hard for Natalie to know if there was still interest in carrying on the conversation. She took a chance. "Did you know there's Braille music, too?"

"I can't imagine!" Bree exclaimed. "I'm still having trouble with the alphabet, never mind *numbers* and *musical notes*."

"I once thought about taking piano lessons," Natalie said, "like maybe when I went to college, because we don't have a piano at home."

"That sounds like a good idea."

Natalie blew the air out of her cheeks and dropped her hands, letting the knitting project rest. "I don't know about college. I always thought I'd go. But now I'm not sure I could get around."

"Come on, Nat, you're so smart!"

"Yeah, well, it used to be part of my dream. In fact, when I was home, this professor we know came over to get some cheese for the holidays. He said I should think about going to Frostburg University where he teaches—it's near my home. At the very least, he said I should visit sometime."

"Then do it!"

"I don't know—"

"Do it, Nat! Maybe I could go, too!"

"There's a thought. We could go together. We could room together!"

Bree seemed really excited. "Do you think so?"

"Why not?"

"Oh, my gosh, Nat. My aunt would be so proud if I went to college!"

Oddly, Bree suddenly grew quiet. "Nat, there is something that I have really wanted to tell you, ever since, like, the first week of school."

"What is it?"

"Do you promise not to tell anyone here?"

"Of course. I promise."

"Not that some people don't know already." Bree hesitated a moment. "But have you ever heard of Space Monkey?"

"Space Monkey," Natalie repeated. At first, she thought it was the name of a rock band, or a rapper, and she wasn't into rap. "No. Who is it?"

But Bree didn't get a chance to answer, because suddenly Serena popped into the open doorway. "What are you guys talking about?"

"College!" Bree said right away, making it pretty clear she didn't want to talk about Space Monkey with Serena.

"Yeah. We were talking about going to college," Natalie agreed.

Serena walked in. Natalie could hear her flip-flops slap across the floor, and felt the bed sink when Serena sat down at the opposite end. "I'm going to college, too," she said. "I'm going to major in psychology. Probably at the community college in Hagerstown. If I can get in."

Eve showed up, too, and said, "Hey, what's up?"

"College. We're talking about going to college," Serena said.

"Really? Who is?" Eve asked.

"Nat and Bree and me," Serena told her.

"Wow," Eve responded. "That's something I could never do."

"Why not?" Natalie asked.

"Too scary," Eve said.

"So what *are* you going to do when you get out of here?" Serena pressed. "Go home to Mommy?"

Natalie cringed.

"Maybe I *will*!" Eve shot back. "And so what if I do? My mom does day care at home. I could help."

"But you don't even like little kids!" Serena reminded her.

Eve didn't reply. She just left, continuing down the hall, her cane tapping lightly, quickly.

Serena's tongue was too quick for her own good sometimes, Natalie thought. When Bree got up and announced she was taking a shower, Serena rose from the end of Natalie's bed and flip-flopped back to her own room. Natalie shook her head and picked up her knitting again, counting the stitches on one needle to see where she was, and thinking that friendships at the Center came with a whole lot of baggage.

It was later in the week that Bree got weird. Really weird. By Teen Group on Thursday, her mood had plunged. She wasn't even speaking to anyone again. Natalie understood how people had their ups and downs, like Paula's blue funk, and Bree had complained about a headache, but there was something more, Natalie could feel it. It seemed to be catching. Sheldon was bummed out at Teen Group, too, although he at least had a reason: one of his friends had just gotten his license. Not even Eve could seem to cheer him up. Driving—and the fact none of the kids here would ever do it—was a tough fact of life for all of them.

"Who cares?" Murph asked in a perky voice. "I don't! Not driving means I don't have to take the driver's test! I won't ever have to pay for car insurance. And I won't ever have to pay for gas—at four dollars a gallon!"

Natalie could tell she was echoing something the social worker had said.

On the way back to the dorm, after Teen Group, Bree called out to Natalie, then grabbed her arm and asked her to step aside for a minute. "Can I talk to you?"

"Sure," Natalie said.

"It's Kirk—my boyfriend."

"What is it?"

"Well, he's pretty upset about me telling him where to get off. He needs to see me immediately, like *now*, or he'll do something drastic."

"Oh, come on, Bree, don't believe that—"

"No. I have to talk to him. He's coming to pick me up right now," she whispered urgently.

"What do you mean *right now*? You can't leave campus on a Thursday afternoon!"

"I know. That's why you can't say anything, Nat. Please. I'm going to go stand by the circle and wait for him. Tell everybody at dinner that I went to the health clinic because I didn't feel good, okay?"

"What if one of the counselors asks me who escorted you?"

"Tell them you took me, okay?"

Natalie did not want to lie.

"*Please.* Just this once. I need to talk to Kirk."

Natalie hated the sound of this plan. But she agreed.

So the deal was this: It was 4 P.M. Natalie would cover for Bree for two hours max. Natalie also agreed to keep her cell phone on, just in case.

She never expected her phone would actually ring (Natalie had set it to vibrate) at five thirty, just as they returned from dinner.

"Bree?" she whispered as soon as she was inside her room.

"Natalie, you need to help me!"

"What's wrong?"

"You need to come and get me, Nat! Please!" she pleaded.

"Where are you?" Natalie asked.

"I'm at that place in the shopping center where you and Arnab ate."

"What? The Parthenon?"

"Yeah. Kirk and I came here and now he's gone. He got ticked off. He said if I was so damned independent with my stupid cane, I could find my own way back to school. But I can't. You know I can't. But you have that pass, Nat. Can you come and get me?"

"Oh, my God, Bree! I can't walk all the way down there by myself!"

"But you can! That's what that pass is for!"

"Bree, I just got that pass!"

"So it means you can do it!"

"But it's getting late."

"Yeah! Since when does *that* make a difference? Come on, Natalie! They'll kick me out of school if they find out I left. If you come, we can both walk back together. And if you do it now, we can be back in an hour. No one will even know we were gone."

Natalie held the phone away from her ear. She tried to envision walking all the way down to the shopping center. She would follow the driveway and turn left at Dunbar. The intersection at Pace would be scary, but she knew what to do—then the three streets, the utility box, a left into the shopping center . . .

"Please, Natalie. I'm so scared. I don't know what else to do."

"This isn't free time, Bree, you're going to get us both kicked out of school—"

"Nat, you are the only friend I have right now. *Please.*"

Natalie knew this was a bad idea. She could feel it in her gut. On the other hand, maybe it was exactly the kind of thing she needed to do so she wouldn't be afraid the rest of her life. Bree *was* her friend. And Bree needed her. So why not? If those blind teenagers in Tibet could climb a mountain in the Himalayas, Natalie could walk a mile to the Forestville Shopping Center!

Couldn't she?

THE BLIND LEADING THE BLIND

Y ou're nuts!" Serena exclaimed. "You are absolutely insane!"

"Thanks for your confidence," Natalie said. "Look. If I'm not back in two hours, go ahead and tell somebody, okay?"

Leaving the dorm was not hard. A lot of kids went places after dinner. Natalie simply headed down the driveway, hoping that no one would stop and ask her what she was doing out there so late. If they did, she'd tell them she was on her way to the library and got lost. She knew a lot depended on luck. Only one car passed her on the driveway, and it didn't stop.

At Dunbar, Natalie turned left and let her cane follow the edge of grass, shorelining up the hill. At the intersection, she pressed the button and waited for traffic in front of her to stop. Her heart was already thumping double time, but she forced herself to listen carefully. She was so focused that this time she even heard the click of the traffic light changing. It was just past rush hour, so there wasn't a lot of traffic on Dunbar. The cars in front of her came to a halt while cars to her right began moving. She didn't hesitate. If she started thinking about it too much she'd chicken out. Quickly, she tapped three times in front of her and headed out across the road.

When she got to the other side, she heaved a sigh of relief, but kept moving. Up Dunbar. Past the barking dog. When she heard voices approaching, she kept to the left, keeping the arc of her cane as narrow as possible and walking with as much confidence as she could muster. "Good evening," someone said. It was a man's voice. He sounded older, educated, like a nice person. Natalie had to judge quickly. She nodded. "Good evening," she replied, continuing on her way. When she heard his voice moving away, she focused forward again, tripping over the same darn crack in the sidewalk.

A *whap*! against the utility box told her she'd practically made it. So far, so good, she thought. Unbelievable. Natalie couldn't help but smile.

The supermarket was busy. Natalie could hear the jangle of metal carts being pushed over the pavement and smelled the exhaust from cars moving slowly past her. She moved her cane carefully, but still managed to bump into something—a newspaper box? A young woman offered her help. "No thank you," Natalie said. "I'm fine."

Past the liquor store. She heard the rattle of bottles. The nail salon would be next. Yes. The smell of wet polish. Then the Raven's Nest Bar. Natalie heard country music and smelled acrid cigarette smoke. Two men—it sounded like they were outside the bar—were coughing and laughing. There would be two more storefronts before the Parthenon. A bench was to the right of the door. Natalie found the bench, then opened the door. Pizza never smelled so good, she thought.

Inside the restaurant, she stood, unsure of what to do next.

"Bree?" she called softly.

"Natalie! I'm here in the front near a window."

"Keep talking," Natalie said.

"Here. I'm here. I'm standing now. I'm tapping the table."

Natalie heard the *tap, tap, tap*. When she got to Bree, the two girls embraced, and Bree squeezed Natalie's hand. "Thank you so much," she said. "I knew you could do it."

"All right." Natalie was in no mood to chitchat. She knew that probably a good thirty to forty minutes had passed. "Here's what I think we ought to do. Let me sweep with my cane. You hold my left elbow and just do sighted guide. I mean, we can't have two canes out there going at the same time."

"Fine," Bree said. "My bill's paid. Let's go."

"Excuse me." A woman's voice. Close to them. The waitress? "Do you girls want me to call a cab or something?"

Natalie had not even considered that possibility.

"I have, like, two dollars left," Bree said.

Natalie patted her pockets. She hadn't brought a purse. "I don't have any money at all," she said, suddenly regretting it. A cab would have been a good idea. But which cab company to call? She'd overheard Miss Karen talking about cabs one day, how she always used the same company and asked for Len or Jerry, because she knew they wouldn't cheat her. But Natalie wouldn't have a clue what cab company to call.

"We'll be fine," Natalie said. "Thanks. We don't have far to go."

"You're sure?" the young woman sounded concerned. "I can call the school for you."

"No!" Natalie responded. "Please don't! We're supposed to be doing this on our own. Really, it's no problem," she assured her.

The smell of beer and smoke quickly identified the bar as the girls headed back down the sidewalk.

"Hey, lookee there." A man's loud, husky voice. "Where you girls headed?"

Judging from the sound of his voice, Natalie figured he was standing in the bar's doorway.

The girls ignored the question and walked by.

"That there," the man joked, "is the blind leading the blind." He and another man laughed heartily.

Cruel comment, but it was true, wasn't it? It *was* the blind leading the blind. And they were doing just fine.

In front of the supermarket, Natalie bumped into an empty food cart and set it rolling. She tried to reach out and stop it, but it got away from her and she had to let it go, cringing when she heard it smash into something. At the entrance to the shopping center, the two girls turned right and walked several blocks down Dunbar. Traffic was light now. Almost no cars at all, which not only meant rush hour was over, but that it was dark out.

Natalie slowed down so she could listen. Then she had a bad feeling and stopped.

"What is it?" Bree asked.

"Shhhh," she said. "Be quiet."

A truck with something rattling in its cargo bay passed them on Dunbar. The sound dissipated as the truck continued down the road. For a while, nothing more—until, from behind them, a cough broke the silence. Then Natalie thought she could smell cigarette smoke.

She swallowed hard and felt in her jacket pocket for the cell phone, knowing that up ahead was the long quiet stretch near the cemetery.

"Natalie, what's wrong?" Bree asked again.

"Let's keep moving," Natalie whispered. "Someone's coming up behind us."

BLINDSIDED

W hat? You think we're being followed?"

"Shhhh!" Natalie warned Bree. "Don't talk so loud!"

"What do we do?"

"I don't know. Just keep walking."

Bree pressed close and her grip tightened, while Natalie's mind spun. Should she yell for help? Blow the whistle attached to her cane? But what if no one heard them?

Keep walking.

Maybe they should wave down a car. But then what if they weren't really being followed? It would be embarrassing. They didn't want to make a scene for nothing.

Keep walking.

Was she trying to talk herself out of gut instinct? Weren't you supposed to go with your gut?

Keep walking. Keep walking. It was all Natalie could think to do.

She tried to listen to the sound of her cane on the sidewalk, but it was difficult with her heart pounding in her ears. *Tap, tap, tap.* The cane didn't sound very loud. Did this mean an open space? The stretch of sidewalk past the cemetery? If so, then there wouldn't be any houses close by. No one to hear them scream or see that they were in trouble. Their only hope was that someone would notice them from a passing car. But where was all the traffic she normally heard on Dunbar?

Suddenly, a husky voice behind them said, "Hey there."

Natalie stopped and Bree pressed closed beside her.

"You girls want to join the two of us for a drink?"

Bree tightened her grip around Natalie's arm.

"No. No, thank you," Natalie said firmly, projecting her voice the way Mr. Lee had taught them. *Leave us alone,* she wanted to say, but stopped herself. She didn't want them to know how scared they were.

She started walking again, but then all at once, there were steps. Heavy, rushing steps behind them! Hot breath and an arm around her neck!

"Stop!" Natalie yelled before being jerked viciously backward. The cane flew out of her hand. She grabbed at the arm—it was encased in some sort of fleece—and tried to keep from being choked.

Bree screamed, and Natalie felt her kick as they were pulled apart.

Scared, Natalie tried to think, but in her panic all she could do was yell and scream.

"Let go!" she hollered.

"Behave yourself and no one gets hurt!" the man told her.

"No! Let go!" she screamed again. Natalie knew she had to fight back. She lifted one leg from the ground and tried to stomp on the man's foot, but he moved too quickly and Natalie lost her balance. "Let go of me!"

Why wasn't a car stopping?

The hold tightened around her neck. She needed to hook her chin inside the top of his forearm so he couldn't cut off her air. She dug her chin in hard. It was supposed to be uncomfortable for him because of the pressure on his radial nerve.

It worked! His arm eased its hold on Natalie's neck and she didn't waste time. She threw her head back, trying to smash him in the face, but the move backfired. Angry, the man grunted and put his arm around her neck even tighter so she couldn't push her chin inside. He reeked of beer and smoke and perspiration. Natalie struggled to breathe. Then, with all the strength she could muster, she used both hands to yank down on the man's arm and sank her teeth deep into the exposed skin near his wrist.

"You bitch!" he hollered, wincing in pain. He slapped the side of Natalie's head with one hand and, as he did, his grip loosened and Natalie wriggled away. In her split second of freedom, she whirled around and sent her right fist flying in an arc toward what she dearly hoped was the man's upper lip. Forget the Universal Reference Point. Mr. Lee had told them there was a nerve where the upper lip meets the bottom of the nose, and if she could hit it with enough force she could knock a full-grown man unconscious.

Just like in practice in the gym, Natalie kept her wrist straight so she wouldn't break it and aimed the ridge of knuckles for the nerve point, pivoting her hips as she swung and driving the swing all the way through. She didn't think about it—she just did it. And she made contact all right. Pain shot back through her hand and into her arm.

"Aaaahhh!" the man hollered.

A good, strong hit, even if it did feel more like the side of his nose than an upper lip. But it didn't knock him out, or even knock him down.

"Damn you!" The man's hand struck Natalie hard in the face and sent her wheeling backward to the ground. She scrambled to get away, but he grabbed her ankle, then her hand, and yanked her to her feet, nearly pulling her arm out of its socket. Something warm trickled out of her nose.

"Stop!" she yelled again as he gripped both her hands at the wrists. "Leave me alone!"

"Damn!" he cried, twisting her wrists painfully. "My nose!"

Surprisingly, he let go of one of her hands, and as soon as he did, Natalie swung her right foot back and kicked the man as hard as she could. She was going for the groin but got his knee instead. Not a bad hit, though. He crumpled in pain, letting go of her other wrist.

"Help!" she screamed again.

A car's horn blared.

"Bree!" Natalie cried.

"What's going on?" a voice called out.

"Help!" Natalie yelled. "Help us! We're being attacked!"

The horn blared again.

"I've got the police on the phone!" a voice shouted from the darkness.

"Eddy, out of here!" yelled the man who had attacked Natalie.

Another voice several yards away replied, "Split?"

The men took off.

But where was Bree? Why wasn't she yelling or saying anything?

Natalie dropped down on all fours and used her hands to search for her cane. "Bree?" she called, running her hands over the rough cement sidewalk and the grass to one side.

She found her cane and stood.

"Bree!" she called again.

A faint voice in the darkness. "Over here!"

"Where?"

"Here!"

The stranger with a younger man's voice came from the other direction. "Are you all right? Those guys are gone. What happened?"

"I can't find my friend," Natalie cried.

"Oh, my gosh, you're blind! Are you both blind?" the young man asked incredulously.

The young man gave Natalie a handkerchief, which she pressed to her nose. He led her to Bree, who was sitting nearby. Natalie collapsed on the ground beside her. Natalie's cheek stung, and her nose and mouth were sticky with blood. She could taste it. Her right hand throbbed. She put an arm around Bree, and the two girls hugged and cried.

Within a few minutes, police sirens pierced the night. Natalie actually thought she could see a slight glimmer of their swirling lights.

Bree was shaking and sucking in breath. "I really hit my head . . . that guy swung me so hard."

"Thank you for stopping," Natalie said aloud, not knowing exactly where the young man stood. "You saved us."

"I got a good one in, Nat," Bree said. "I hit that guy hard in the Adam's apple and almost got away. But then he came after me again and threw me on the ground. I've got my purse. It's still here. I don't know where my cane is."

"We'll find it," Natalie said. "Don't worry about your cane. How are you? Are you hurt?"

"I don't feel so good," Bree said. "My head hurts. I really cracked it on something hard when I fell."

"Gosh, Bree. I'm so sorry."

"Hey! Don't *you* be sorry. I shouldn't have asked you to come get me. It was my fault. Everything has been my fault."

"It's okay," Natalie told her.

"But I wanted to tell you—"

"Bree, let's talk later. Just rest for now, okay?"

"Yeah. I need to lie down," Bree said in a whisper. "Just for a minute."

Natalie heard the crackle of a police radio and soon a policeman was kneeling beside her. "Are you all right, miss?"

"I think so," Natalie said. She took the handkerchief away for a moment. "Is my nose still bleeding?"

"Better keep that cloth on it," the officer said.

The young man who had stopped to help gave the police a quick account of what he'd seen. Listening to him, Natalie realized that he must have witnessed almost the entire attack. But two minutes? How could it only have lasted two minutes? It seemed like an eternity!

"I didn't realize what was happening at first," the young man explained. Then he described Natalie's assailant: "A white guy, about five foot eight or nine. Heavyset. Big belly. A beard. A baseball cap. Dark pants, light-colored T-shirt, dark jacket."

"He smelled like beer and cigarettes," Natalie said. "I think he followed us from the bar in the shopping center. The Raven's Nest."

"You're sure?" the officer asked.

Natalie hesitated. "No. I can't be sure. Obviously. But I smelled him. Some guy said something to us when we passed the bar and it was the same voice. He had a fleece jacket on—and he'll have a bite mark near one wrist. I also hit him pretty hard on the nose."

The young man continued, "The other one wasn't as heavy. About the same height."

Natalie spoke up again. "His name was Eddy. The guy who attacked me called him Eddy."

"I didn't get a good look at him," the witness said. "He veered off the sidewalk, toward the woods there."

Woods? There were woods nearby? Natalie put a hand over her eyes.

"I think we'll get you girls down to the hospital to get checked out," the policeman told her.

"I don't think I need a hospital," Natalie said.

"Your friend," he said. "Is she hurt?"

"Bree?" Natalie reached over to touch her arm.

There was no response.

"Bree!"

"Charlie!" the officer hollered. "Call for an ambulance!"

UNEXPECTED TURNS

Serena was only trying to be funny when she saw Natalie's bruised and swollen face the next morning. "You're a sight for sore eyes," she said.

Natalie didn't even try to smile as she readjusted the ice pack on her face. "Is it that bad?"

"Yeah, it's pretty bad. It's a good thing I can't see you any better! But seriously, Nat, you were a real hero," Serena told her as they walked to breakfast.

Eve was just behind them. "I think so, too, Natalie. I would not have been able to do what you did."

Murph struggled to keep up with them. "Yeah, but aren't you going to get in trouble for leaving campus? Why'd you do that anyway?"

Natalie ignored Murph's questions. She was sure there would be repercussions for leaving school, maybe even a suspension—or an expulsion.

In the dining hall, Natalie slumped into a chair at their usual table, folded her cane, and set it beneath the seat. Unable to sleep the night before, she was tired and leaned against the hand that didn't hurt, still keeping the ice pack on her face. Mostly, she worried about Bree.

"What can I get you for breakfast?" Serena asked.

"I don't care. Anything," Natalie said. "Thanks."

Serena returned with a bowl of cereal and a carton of milk and sat down beside Natalie. "I got some Cheerios. Here's a spoon," she said. "Have you heard anything about Bree?"

Natalie took the spoon and shook her head. "Nothing. All I know is that they took her to Johns Hopkins Hospital. I'm going to ask Miss Audra if she'll take me down to visit."

Natalie reached into her pocket for the HOPE stone and hoped with all her heart that nothing serious was wrong with Bree. Then she sat up and tried the other pocket. Several times, she felt both pockets, because they were the same jeans she had worn yesterday. But the little pink stone was gone.

There was no visit with Bree that afternoon. Natalie had to get on the bus and go home to face her parents, who were horrified over what had happened and distressed about how narrowly Natalie had escaped serious harm. The whole weekend turned out to be an exhausting maelstrom of emotion: bouncing from sympathy for Natalie and Bree, to gratitude that everyone was safe, to abject anger at the girls for walking alone at night.

"What were you thinking?" her father demanded. "You could have been killed!"

"I know. I know. It was stupid, a totally stupid thing to do," Natalie agreed with him, over and over. "But Bree begged me to come get her, and somehow I thought I could do it, Dad. But you know something? I did fight off that guy. If Mr. Lee hadn't taught us that self-defense stuff in class, this whole thing might have turned out much differently."

"Mr. Lee, phooey!" her father exclaimed. "Phooey to that whole school! I hate the city. This is why your mother and I live out in the country!"

All weekend, Natalie worried about Bree and was haunted by echoes of the incident. Even just brushing her teeth the first night she was home, she suddenly felt the man's arm around her neck again and sent the toothbrush flying into the sink as her hands instinctually went to her neck. *What did that guy want? Was he going to rob me? What if the man in the car hadn't stopped? What would have happened? I need to thank him. I don't even know who he is. How will I find him?*

Natalie wondered, too, if she would ever have the courage to walk alone again, in public, with just a cane.

She longed for the sympathetic ear of an old friend. She wondered if Meredith even knew what had happened.

A promised call from Miss Audra didn't come until Sunday morning. "Good news," she told Natalie. "The two men who attacked you were caught. They're in jail. You may be asked to identify them by their voices."

"Will Bree and I get kicked out of school, Miss Audra?"

"I don't think so, Natalie. Don't worry about that now."

"How's Bree? When can I see her?"

Miss Audra's disturbing reply: "Let's wait until you're back, okay?"

Early Monday morning, snow started falling in Baltimore. It was the first snow of the season in the eastern part of the state, and kids at school were excited. No one seemed to be dwelling on the incident from the previous week, and no one else seemed concerned that one student wasn't in class that morning. Instead, there was endless silly talk about how much snowfall was predicted and speculation over what was required to close school and send them home.

"Let's turn our pajamas inside out tonight!" Murph suggested at lunch, instigating a round of laughter.

"I haven't done that since I was, like, in third grade," Serena said.

Natalie sat silently.

In American government, Mr. Joe had a new assignment. "On June 26, 2008," he said, "the Supreme Court struck down the District of Columbia's ban on handgun possession and decided for the first time in our nation's history that the Second Amendment guarantees an individual's right to own a gun for self-defense.

"This decision," he went on, "wiped away years of lower court decisions that held that the intent of the amendment, ratified more than two hundred years ago, was to tie the right of gun possession to militia service. How do you feel about this? Sheldon, go ahead."

"I don't think anybody should have a gun," he said. "There is too much violence in this country—in this city! Baltimore has one of the highest homicide rates in the country. And Washington, D.C., is not much better. They need to keep guns off the street!"

"I agree," Murph added. "Guns are bad."

"My uncle got shot last year and he wasn't doing anything," JJ jumped in to say. "He was just standing outside on the street is all. Somebody drove by and shot him."

"Hands, people. Remember to raise your hand and let me call on you before speaking out," Mr. Joe reminded them. "Serena, go ahead."

"I think the government should take away all the guns," she said, "and throw them in the ocean."

"*All* the guns? Okay. Does anybody here have a different opinion?" Mr. Joe asked.

Natalie, who didn't feel like participating in any discussions that morning, nevertheless raised her hand.

"Natalie, go ahead."

"I just want to point out that farmers like my dad need guns to protect their animals and their land. We have a gun safe in my house with several rifles and shotguns in it."

She heard a couple gasps in the room.

"I've fired a gun myself," she said, unashamed. "I learned how to use a shotgun when I was eight years old. But you've got to understand that back where I live, hunting is a big deal. Wild turkey, deer—there's even a black bear season—"

"Oh, my gosh!" Murph interrupted. "Bears are so cute! How can anyone kill a cute little bear?"

Murph was behind her somewhere. Natalie turned around in her seat. "My father would shoot a black bear in a heartbeat if it was coming after our goats," she said.

Just then, the door to the classroom opened and Mark, the student with tattoos up and down his arms, rolled his wheelchair out of the room, letting the door slam behind him.

"Mark!" Mr. Joe hollered after him. "Just a minute there, young man, you can't—"

"Mr. Joe!" Sheldon called out, stopping the teacher in mid-sentence. Sheldon lowered his voice. "Mr. Joe, you're new, so maybe you don't know. But Mark is in that chair because of a bullet. It went in his head. Paralyzed and blinded him both. His own cousin did it. They were foolin' around with somebody's gun."

For a long moment, Mr. Joe remained silent. Natalie heard him pull out his chair and sit down. "Thank you for explaining," he said quietly. He moved some papers on his desk while the class waited.

"Well," he finally said to the class, "life's journey can be full of unexpected turns. I would like you all to reflect and examine your thoughts on this issue. Two pages due the first week of January after the holiday break. Decide which way you would have voted if you were one of the Supreme Court judges."

In gym, the girls shot baskets at a hoop equipped with a buzzer that sounded when the ball hit the rim. Mr. Lee was sick, so self-defense class had been canceled. Just as well, Natalie thought. They would probably be rehashing the incident of last week.

Eager for news of Bree, Natalie rushed from the gym to Miss Audra's office.

"Hey there," Miss Audra said. She gave Natalie a small hug. "Your face looks better already. The swelling has really gone down, Natalie."

"How's Bree?" Natalie asked. She put her backpack on the floor and, feeling for a chair, sat down, still holding her cane. "Can we go to the hospital?"

She heard Miss Audra close the door. It seemed to take forever for her to return and sit opposite Natalie. Why wasn't Miss Audra saying anything? Was she gearing up to tell Natalie that they were revoking her Forestville pass because of the trouble? Or was she about to break the news that they were suspending—or expelling—them both from school?

Instead, Miss Audra, in a calm voice, asked Natalie a weird question. "Do you know what an aneurysm is?"

"An aneurysm?" Natalie asked.

"Yes."

"Some kind of a disease?"

"Not exactly," Miss Audra replied. "An aneurysm is a weak or thin spot on a blood vessel that balloons out and fills with blood."

Natalie frowned and sat up. "Does this have something to do with Bree?"

"Yes," Miss Audra confirmed. "It does."

"She has one of these, Miss Audra? An aneurysm? Where?"

"In her neck," Miss Audra said.

"Is she going to be all right?"

She heard Miss Audra sigh. "This is going to be so hard," she began, "because I know that Bree was your roommate and your friend—"

Natalie's cane fell to the floor as she gripped the armrests on the chair. "Miss Audra, wait—"

But Miss Audra continued. "The aneurysm burst, Natalie. There were *huge* efforts to save her—"

"Wait a minute! Wait a minute! Stop!" Natalie implored, even putting her hands up to her ears.

But Miss Audra would not be stopped. Gently, she pulled Natalie's hands from her ears. "Bree has passed on," she said. "I'm so sorry, Natalie. There was nothing anyone could do."

SIGHT UNSEEN

Passed on? What? Did she mean dead?

A chill ran through Natalie. It felt as thought someone had tapped an icicle through the top of her head and driven it straight down through her core.

"Bree is *dead*, Miss Audra?" Natalie couldn't quite grasp it. It was like a bad dream, or a nightmare. Surely, she misunderstood.

Miss Audra moved beside Natalie and put an arm around her shoulders. "She died early Sunday morning, Nat. No one told me until last night."

"Bree is gone?" Natalie asked again, still in disbelief.

"Yes. I'm afraid so."

Natalie's eyes began to fill with tears, and yet she didn't cry, not really, because it still seemed so unreal. Shock. Maybe that's what shock was like.

Miss Audra plucked Kleenex from a container behind her and pressed the tissues into Natalie's hands.

"I'm not sure how much you know, Natalie, about Bree's situation. As teachers we're not supposed to share this information with other students."

Natalie wiped off some of the tears that began trickling down her cheek. "She was in an accident. That's about all I know. I think her boyfriend was driving the car."

Miss Audra didn't respond right away. "Well, she wasn't exactly in an accident so much as she caused one."

Natalie turned her head slightly. "What do you mean?"

She could hear Miss Audra take in another breath and let it out. "I don't know how much I should say, but it was in the newspapers some months ago. Last spring, Natalie, Bree hanged herself."

"What?! She tried to kill herself?"

"No. This is why it was an accident. She was trying to get high by cutting off her own air supply. You may have heard of this. It's called the choking game, the fainting game, the something dreaming game—"

"Space Monkey?" Natalie cut in.

"Yes. I think that's one of the names, too."

Natalie bit her bottom lip and held her face in her hands. This is what Bree had started to tell her.

"Bree was doing this—this *thing*—to herself to get high. She had a scarf and had tied it to the bed. . . . From what I understand, she passed out and her own body weight strangled her. Her boyfriend found her. He untied the scarf and saved her life, no question about it. But her brain had already been deprived of oxygen and there was some damage."

Natalie brought her hands down. "To her eyes?"

"Actually, no. Her eyes weren't damaged. It was her brain. The lack of oxygen damaged parts of her brain."

"But she went blind!"

"Yes. But remember, Natalie, the eyes are our camera, the brain is our TV. If something happens to that place in our brain where the messages are received, the image can't be seen."

Natalie stared into the void that seemed so much darker now.

"It's also why she had seizures," Miss Audra added.

"Is that what killed her then? A seizure?"

"No," Miss Audra replied. "It's pretty complicated. . . . When Bree tied that scarf around her neck, she compressed the carotid artery in her neck and created the conditions for an aneurysm, that little bulge I talked about. Her aunt says she had been complaining of headaches recently. It was probably a clue that something wasn't right."

"Yes. She did have headaches."

"The fall she took the other night disturbed that aneurysm and caused it to burst. That's what killed her, Natalie."

"I never should have gone to get her—"

"Don't you dare start blaming yourself!" Miss Audra demanded as Natalie covered her face with her hands. "Don't go there!"

But Natalie knew it was her fault. She had summoned the courage to go get Bree, but the effort had backfired. Everything was worse because of it. Worse in a way that could never be undone.

The next three days were surreal. It seemed when Natalie took another full breath, she was already in her own room back in western Maryland, driven there by her parents. "I just want to go home," she had told them after visiting the funeral parlor to say good-bye to Bree. "Please come and get me." So they did. But Natalie had barely spoken on the long ride home. She sat in the backseat with her head on a pillow propped against the side window. Her hands were in her lap, holding the teddy bear Meredith had given her and an uneaten sandwich in a Ziploc bag.

It wasn't that Bree was such a great friend, Natalie thought. They barely knew each other, after all. But there was so much they had in common, so many challenges they could have faced and overcome together, and they were becoming closer. It was, Natalie realized, the potential friendship that she mourned as well as the horror of what had happened. Bree's death was the culmination of many bad things. It was difficult for Natalie to sift through the fragments of recent memory and isolate what bothered her most.

Scenes from the previous day's events replayed in her head as well: Miss Audra, escorting her to the funeral home . . . Natalie, sitting numbly in the car, still trying to understand. "Why? Why would Bree do that?"

"Only Bree could tell you that, Natalie, and she's not here now," Miss Audra had said. "But this *thing* she did—passing out for fun— was a way of getting high, of temporarily escaping from the world. Friends at school did it and wanted her to do it, too. So there was some peer pressure. Even her boyfriend pushed her."

"But *why*, Miss Audra? Why would Bree want to choke herself and risk doing all that damage?" Natalie opened her hands and leaned forward in the car seat, pushing against the seat belt.

"She probably didn't ever consider the consequences if something went wrong, Natalie. It's like teenagers binge drinking or driving too fast. They don't think anything bad is ever going to happen—not to *them*."

Natalie leaned back in her seat and sighed. "I still don't get it."

"No," Miss Audra agreed. "No. A lot of us don't understand. That's what makes it so hard."

At the funeral parlor, organ music, soft voices, and the smell of flowers had surrounded Natalie like a dream. Miss Audra led her to a table and described the photographs displayed. "Gabriella's first recital," she read from a note. "Miss Peggy's Dance Studio."

"What does she look like in the picture, Miss Audra?"

"She's cute. About four years old. Wearing a pink leotard, pink tights—and not ballet slippers, but tap shoes, I think. Her hair is short, with bangs. She's smiling. Big smile."

When they approached Bree's casket, a woman introduced herself as Gabriella's aunt and said, "You must be Natalie from school."

"Yes," Natalie replied.

The woman took Natalie's hand and pressed it. "I want you to know, Natalie, that Bree was very fond of you. You made a difference in her life, a big difference in a short period of time. I think she wanted to be like you. She was finally turning a huge corner in her life."

Natalie swallowed hard. She did not want to cry in front of Bree's aunt.

"Take care of yourself," the aunt had told her. "I hope you live out the dreams that you and Bree shared."

Natalie was glad she couldn't see Bree in her casket, laid out, Natalie heard, in a pretty blue dress, with pairs of tap and ballet shoes tucked in at her feet. Nodding her head to say a prayer, and good-bye, Natalie hoped that somehow, somewhere, Bree was in a better place, and that in this better place, Bree could dance—and, perhaps, even see again.

At home, Natalie went to her room right away and closed her door. She reached into her pocket to rub the pink stone, forgetting she had lost it, and sat on the edge of her bed. Belongings from school were in a heap on the small wooden desk against the wall. "Take the Brailler home with you," Miss Karen had insisted. "Get some practice in over the holidays." The vacation from school wasn't for another two weeks, but Natalie's parents said that, given what had happened, she needed the extra time at home.

"The break will be good for you," Miss Audra said. "Please try to enjoy the holidays. We'll look forward to starting over in the new year."

Everyone was nice. They were giving her space—*time to grieve,* as Ms. Kravitz put it. Natalie appreciated all their efforts. She did. But nothing they said made any difference. Not really. Because why would she want to continue at a place where she had failed so miserably? The damage had been done. She had no intention of ever going back to the Baltimore Center for the Blind.

Not in January.

Not ever.

⠿

LIVING SCARED

At home, Natalie's parents tried to cheer her up. They cut an early Christmas tree, dragged it through the woods, and set it up in the front room, festooning it with colored lights, balls, and silver tinsel. The tree's smell brought back good memories. But when Natalie touched its prickly branches and felt the familiar ornaments, it made her sad not to be able to see them.

Mostly, Natalie hung out in her room, sleeping, sometimes putting on music, sometimes not. Often, she simply lay on her bed, listening to the clank of the radiator and staring at nothing because there was nothing to stare at. She didn't even want to go out to the barn to visit pregnant Nuisance, because she couldn't tell the goats apart.

For two whole weeks she stayed in the house. No one called. No one left a message. *Out of sight, out of mind,* she figured. She felt abandoned by Meredith, and every time she thought about Bree, Natalie wondered if part of her own self had died, too.

When the mantel clock downstairs chimed eight o'clock one evening, Natalie was reminded of the bluebird on Eve's clock. The bluebird sang at eight, followed by the red-winged blackbird at nine. . . . Paula would be recharging the battery to her wheelchair and laying out her clothes on the mat beside her bed. . . . The kids at school would be moving on without her.

Sometimes she heard Miss Audra's voice: *Will you utilize the skills you are learning here to go out and embrace the world? Or will you go home to Mom and Dad and hide out, living scared?* The questions made her angry. The world had been cruel to her, hadn't it? She didn't want any part of it.

"I'm not going back to Baltimore, to school," she declared one evening. Neither of her parents argued nor questioned her decision.

Her parents were busy, going about their daily chores. She heard them rise at the crack of dawn, her father out the door to start the milking. A big truck came and went, probably delivering goat milk from the Amish farm. Her father had had to reach out for more milk now that the cheese was finding a larger market. Every three days, a tanker brought several hundred gallons of milk, paid for by the pound, from local Amish farms.

A multitude of tasks kept her mother hopping: making meals, keeping house, packaging cheese, and working in the office, where she took orders and sent bills. But she made time for Natalie, too, and was always there, eager to cook an egg or make a sandwich whenever Natalie came downstairs.

Her father tried to get her out of the house. "Let's take a walk," he suggested one day after the three of them had eaten lunch together. "We've had a bear hanging out and I want to check the fence lines. Why don't you come with me?"

"A bear?" Natalie asked. "Aren't they supposed to be hibernating?"

"Not if they're getting easy food. They don't hibernate 'cause of the weather, you know. But because food gets scarce."

Natalie didn't know that. Still, her reply was sarcastic. "I'd be a terrific help, wouldn't I? Stumbling around the fields with my cane."

Her father didn't even reply. She heard his heavy boots move across the kitchen tiles and out the back door. She could still hear them as he pounded down the steps and started across the yard. *He* was the one so eager to have her come home. She bet he was sorry now.

Natalie, still in her pajamas at noon, remained sitting at the kitchen table with her mother. Neither one of them said anything. Natalie's cold fingers curled around a mug of hot tea. She knew that she cowered in a stew of self-pity, anger—and fear. But how could anyone expect her to go out into the world after what had happened? She didn't want to be a victim again. Nothing was worth that. So what if she lived at home? So what if her parents helped her? They *wanted* to help!

Guilt was part of it, too: if she hadn't made that walk to get Bree, if someone else had gone to pick her up in a car—they could have called Miss Audra! Or if they'd taken a taxi, then Bree would be alive. Doctors could have fixed the bulge in her artery before it burst. They could be friends, planning a future together.

What a mess. Sometimes, Natalie came close to feeling that she did not want to be around at all. It frightened her because she had never felt that way before. But now, immersed in darkness, she felt she had sunk to the lowest point of her life with nothing to offer, and nothing to work toward in the future.

"The cat's back," her mother said, out of the blue, out of nowhere as they sat opposite each other at the kitchen table.

Natalie frowned. "What cat?"

"The cat who waits for scraps! He was there this morning, at the milk room door."

"Really?" Natalie replied, surprised because the cat had disappeared weeks ago.

Her mother got up and pushed her chair in. "He looks a little beat up if you ask me. I brought some egg and toast out and Dad poured a little warm milk over it." She put her dish in the sink and ran the water a second. "When I checked later, the plate was licked clean. He was pretty hungry, I guess. Maybe you could take something out to him tomorrow."

Ah. Another ploy to get her outside the house. Natalie turned her head slightly. "Yeah, maybe," she said.

"Well, I'll leave the old pie tin beside the dish drainer if you feel like it. I really don't have time to be doing that."

She bent to kiss Natalie on the head as she passed by. "Got to get back to work."

The next morning, after she heard both her parents leave the house to work in the barn, Natalie rose and pulled on jeans and a sweatshirt. She did her eyedrops and went downstairs, patting her hands across the kitchen counter until she found the pie tin beside the dish drainer. It was already loaded with toast scraps and what felt like an entire scrambled egg. Natalie shook off the egg that stuck to her fingertips and had to smile. So her mother liked the cat, too. Quickly, she found a jacket and some gloves, then took the food and, with her cane, made her way out the back door and down the two steps to the yard. The air was cold and prickled her nose. She thought she could smell the coming snow. Beneath her feet, the ground was frozen, a little icy in spots. Natalie's footsteps crunched as she made her way slowly, carefully.

As she approached the barn, she could hear the cat meow, and the sound helped guide her to the right spot. "It's okay," she said softly, "I've got some breakfast for you."

When her cane hit the cement stoop to the milking parlor, she turned around and sat down, carefully placing the pie tin beside her. "Come on," she urged gently. "I won't hurt you."

But the wait became a long one and the cement steps grew hard. The cold was getting to her as well. A few flakes of snow landed on her face and melted, pooling and trickling down her warm cheeks. The cat meowed, but wouldn't come any closer. It was, Natalie realized, living scared. Just like her.

That same afternoon, when Natalie was fixing another cup of tea, her mother came in from the creamery. "I'm kind of in a pinch," she said, stomping new snow from her boots and rubbing her hands together to get warm. "Do you think you could help me wrap some cheese for a big order?"

Natalie squeezed the tea bag and set it on a dish. "I guess so. If you want."

Immediately, her mother put her to work out in the creamery, setting up a small assembly line where Natalie could wrap small trapezoids of goat blue cheese in sheets of plastic, press a label on the package, and stack the cheese on a large tray beside her.

There was a flicker of good feeling about the work. Natalie was using her hands to get something done, and it was helping her parents make money. The work didn't require much thinking and she didn't have to deal with people. Maybe, she thought, this could be her job. She could live at home and wrap cheese. She might even be able to take orders over the phone. She knew her way around the house, the creamery, and the barn. She could even visit with Nuisance now that the mother-to-be with her bulging sides was protected in her own pen. Staying home and making cheese would be uncomplicated—and, best of all, it would be *safe*.

"Great job, Nat," her mother said, piling up the wrapped cheese in her arms.

"I should have offered earlier," Natalie said.

Over the next few days, a routine developed. Natalie rose with her parents, had breakfast with them, and took some food out to the cat. On the third morning, she tried holding out a toast crust and was surprised to feel it suddenly disappear with a small, quick motion.

A full morning of work wrapping and labeling cheese in the creamery was followed by a visit to Nuisance and a new game called Find the Biscuit. Natalie would hide the treat in a different jacket pocket each time, and Nuisance would have to push her nose into each one until she found it. After lunch, Natalie would return to the creamery to help some more.

The radio was usually on while Natalie and her mother worked. They took turns choosing the station, switching from rock and country to her mother's golden oldies. Sometimes they talked. And one afternoon, Natalie's mother mentioned school. "If you're not going back to Baltimore," she said, "you need to be thinking of how you'll continue your education."

"I've already thought about it," Natalie said. "We could talk to Mrs. Russell, my old vision teacher. Maybe she can come to the house so I can work from home."

"I should put in a call to her then," Natalie's mother said.

"Yeah, I guess so."

Why not? Why wouldn't that work? Natalie wondered. She placed another trapezoid of goat blue cheese on the tray and pressed a homemade Mountainside Farm label onto its top.

"Oh—I ran into Meredith and her father at the food store,"

Natalie's mother went on, taking an armful of wrapped cheese into the walk-in refrigerator for storage. She called back over her shoulder, "They didn't know you were home. I suggested Meredith come over sometime and you two could watch a movie or something."

Natalie stopped wrapping. "You're kidding, right?"

The heavy door to the refrigerator clicked shut. "No," her mother replied.

Natalie lifted her chin. "Why did you do that? I don't want to see Meredith. I don't want to see anyone. Oh, I forgot. I can't *see* anyone anyway. But you know, Mom, maybe I just want to be left alone."

Her mother's voice was calm. She returned and stood close to Natalie. "You've been home more than two weeks now, Natalie. Even your father says it's time to get out more, or have a friend over. You're totally isolating yourself—"

"Yeah, well, maybe that's what I want!"

"I was just thinking—"

"Well, stop thinking!" Natalie slammed her hand on the table. "I'm blind, Mom. Can't you frickin' see that? I'm not like everybody else anymore. Why would they want to spend time with me? I can't *do* the things they do!"

Her mother did not back off. "Come on. Get over it, Natalie. Lots of people lose their sight. It doesn't mean they go hide and drop out of life! Look at your Braille teacher. You told me she takes two buses and walks the last mile to school. She took a plane to New Mexico for Thanksgiving. You do what you have to do, and you move on."

"Easy for you to say!" Natalie shot back angrily.

"The school was *preparing* you, Natalie."

"For what? So I wouldn't be *blindsided by blindness*?"

The smallest hesitation. "Well—yes," her mother affirmed quietly.

"Yeah, well, let me tell you something, Mom. No one can ever be prepared to go blind. No one! Not ever!" And with that, Natalie got up from the table, grabbed her cane, and yanked it open so hard she broke off the bottom segment. "Shit! Now look what you made me do!"

"Natalie!"

"Just leave me alone! I hate you!" She threw the rest of the cane on the floor and stormed out of the creamery. With her arms flailing, she knocked a bag of curds onto the floor and heard them hit the cement floor with a sickening splat. There was probably fifteen pounds worth of cheese in that bag. Natalie fled the creamery and groped for the door, eager to get out. It was somewhere on her left, but where? Running her hands along the wall, she kept moving until she was in a corner. A corner? What corner was that?!

Natalie held her face in her hands and tried to stop herself. What was happening? It wasn't like her to yell like that—or to cuss at her mother. She knew she'd been unfair, once again blaming the person who had always been her biggest supporter—*her mother*—because it was so easy, and because her mother always pushed her to do the right thing. When the tears came, Natalie didn't even try to stop them.

Crying, she squatted headfirst into the cobwebs of the corner and didn't flinch when her mother came from behind and wrapped her arms around her. "It's okay," her mom assured her. "It's okay."

STARTING FROM THE EDGES

The main shaft of Natalie's cane had a dent and some scratches from when it had fallen on the sidewalk during the attack in Baltimore. Natalie touched the sad reminders as her mother laid out the broken cane on the kitchen table like a wounded soldier and measured it. Afterward, her mother called the school and asked them to ship a replacement. When they finished, Natalie gathered the cane's broken pieces, took them upstairs, and gently set the loose bundle on her bookshelf.

Christmas came and went. Natalie enjoyed opening the gifts she received, mostly clothes, new hats and gloves, a pair of fur-lined moccasins, a blank journal for writing poetry, although how could she now? Didn't her parents think of that? She could write poetry in Braille, she supposed. But anyway, she hadn't been writing poetry anymore.

Natalie didn't have any gifts to give and regretted not finishing the blue scarf she had been knitting for her mother. So many things, she thought, remained undone.

With the holidays came another foot of new snow, and in the days that followed, Natalie stayed inside except for the daily morning walk (fifty-eight steps through the shoveled path) to the barn, where she sat on the step, huddled against the cold, and held out pieces of toast to the cat, who snatched the food and ran away. She had stopped working in the creamery. And her mother had stopped asking for help.

When school started again in January, Serena called Natalie. "It's boring here without you," she said. "Well, I take that back. It's boring here even with you!" She laughed. "But you did spice things up, Nat. . . . You even got Eve excited about going to college. She doesn't want anything to do with day care anymore. . . . Hey, you're coming back, aren't you? I mean, you're not crapping out on us. We'll come out and get you, you know. We'll *haunt* you!"

The call made Natalie smile, even if she did evade the questions.

Then Arnab called. "Just wondering how you were doing," he said so politely. Soon, Natalie found herself deep in a discussion of goat cheese production. "First, all the milk goes into a holding tank," Natalie told him. "How much? It holds about a thousand gallons. . . . Yeah, it's huge. From there, the milk goes into a pasteurizer, which heats up the milk. . . . Arnab! Of course I know. It's heated to a hundred and fifty degrees and held there for thirty minutes. After it's cooled down, we add bacteria. The kind and the amount of bacteria determine the kind of cheese we make. . . . That's right. It's basically controlled spoilage of milk." They laughed.

"Yes," Natalie assured him. "I'm looking forward to being with you again, too." She didn't tell him she wouldn't be returning.

Finally the new cane arrived. Natalie opened the package herself and carefully lifted the cane out of its protective bubble wrap. She unfolded it and felt it from the grip on down. The segments were smooth and slick, the metal tip simple and straight. The new cane seemed lighter somehow. She tried it out in the backyard, and now that some of the snow had melted, she was able to follow the edge of the yard up to the barn and didn't need to count steps. She could hear the drip of melting icicles and held her face up to the sun, it felt so good.

Opening the barn door, Natalie surprised her mother in the creamery. "Can I help you wrap cheese?" she asked.

Mrs. Russell was finally in touch late one afternoon by phone. She said she was glad to help Natalie, but she would not be able to make home visits. "Will you be enrolling at the high school?"

"No," Natalie said quickly. "I'm going to work from home."

"Well, dear. I'll do what I can. Let's meet one day after school. How about Thursday? I'll meet you in the school library after classes."

Natalie did not want to go to the high school, but what choice did she have? Thursday at the high school. Ugh. Something *more* to worry about, because she didn't want to *go* anywhere, or be seen by anyone.

"Look, you're the one who wanted to stay home, Natalie. If Mrs. Russell can only meet you at school, then that is where you'll have to go." They were in the creamery together, working. Natalie's mother was sliding clean, empty trays onto the shelves of a tall, rolling cart. Natalie could tell the trays were empty from the rattling sound they made and the speed with which her mother worked. They would fill those trays with chunks of cheese now sitting in a tub of brine and push the cart into the aging room.

"I can't teach you Braille, Nat. Never mind all the work that would be involved with homeschooling. I don't know how we'd handle that."

Natalie dropped her head. It wasn't going to be so easy then.

"I wouldn't worry about going over to the high school," her

mother tried to tell her. "It's after school when everyone's gone. It'll be fine." Natalie was silent. When they finished loading the trays, she slumped back in her chair while the cart was noisily rolled away.

When her mother returned, she sat down. Natalie heard the scrape of the chair, the intake of breath, and the sigh. She was either tired or getting ready to say something, Natalie figured.

"Do you remember that trip we took to Bethany Beach last year?" her mother asked.

Natalie's head popped up. "How could I forget *that*?"

"Oh, come on. Was it that bad?"

"Mom! I mean, first of all, Dad never should have gone, because he worried about the farm the entire time. Plus, he hates just sitting around doing nothing. He doesn't much like to read, so what was there for him to do on the beach? I felt bad for him."

"He did it for *you*, though. He wanted you to have the experience of seeing the ocean, and he wanted us to make the trip as a family."

"All of which I appreciated," Natalie insisted. "But it was so *awful*. Not just the thing with Dad, but when you made me go in that water. It scared me to death. I still have nightmares, do you know that?"

"Nightmares about the ocean?"

"Yes!"

"You said you wanted to know what it was like!" her mother reminded her.

"Yeah, but I changed my mind and you wouldn't let me go back!"

"Gosh, Natalie. You know how to swim—and we weren't out that far."

"But then that wave hit and you let go of my hand!"

"It was not a very big wave—"

"It knocked me down, Mom! I couldn't see! I was under that water and it was dark. It scared me!"

"Yes," her mother said calmly, "and then what happened?"

"What do you mean 'what happened'?"

"What happened next? Did you drown?"

Natalie paused. "*Nooo*. I didn't drown. Obviously."

"So what happened?"

Natalie frowned. She was irritated by the question even as she reflected on the brief, but intense, panic, the struggle to get herself upright after she was rolled around by the wave, the water in her ears and eyes, the sand in her hair, the hard pebbles beneath her feet, the coughing . . .

"What happened?" her mother pressed.

Natalie shrugged. "I got my footing and walked out."

"Yes," her mother said. "*You got your footing and you walked out.*"

The first thing Natalie heard when she returned to Western Allegany High School Thursday afternoon were the sounds of basketball practice, the whistle and the squeak of sneakers against the wooden floor in the gym as they echoed down the empty hallways. Natalie found it odd and unsettling to be using her cane in such familiar territory. She tried to limit the arc of her swing so she wouldn't whack the cane into the wall or the metal lockers as she and her mother made their way to the library.

Mrs. Russell greeted her with an enormous hug. Natalie filled her in on what she had learned at the Center for the Blind, and then they outlined some of the techniques they would work on together, starting with Braille.

"If it's possible," Natalie said, "I'd like to learn how to use the JAWS program on the computer so I can do research—and so I can e-mail my friends back in Baltimore. Some of them don't have cell phones."

Mrs. Russell hesitated before replying. "I'm sorry, Natalie. I don't have that program here."

"Couldn't the school get it?" Natalie asked.

"Probably not," Mrs. Russell said. "At least not this year. It would be a big item for the budget. It would have to be approved by the county's Board of Education and, with all the budget cuts, I'm not optimistic."

Natalie was stunned, although she should have known.

"That's where you're going to miss out, Natalie," Mrs. Russell noted. "I can't give you the technology training you could have gotten at the school in Baltimore."

Although disappointed, Natalie and her mother thanked Mrs. Russell and, after putting their coats back on, set out down the hall.

"Oh! I forgot!" Her mother stopped. "I needed Mrs. Russell to sign these papers. Wait here, Nat, I'll be right back."

"But—"

"I'll be right back!"

Natalie held the cane in front of her and stood stiffly, taking in and letting out a deep breath. *Hurry up,* she mouthed silently to her mother.

But her mother wasn't fast enough. Voices were coming up the hall from the other direction. Kids' voices. Natalie tensed up.

One voice said, "Thanks for coming." Two voices chimed together: "Sure. See you tomorrow." Then one set of footsteps came closer.

"Nat! Hey! I thought that was you! It's Jake!"

Unbelievable. Jake was always popping up! Natalie turned toward his voice with a tentative smile, and before she knew it, she was swallowed up in Jake's warm embrace—with the cane sandwiched between them. What a surprise! She couldn't be sure, but it felt as though he was taller. And was it possible he'd lost that big stomach he had?

"It is so great to see you back in school!" he exclaimed, releasing her.

"Jake! Yes! Thank you. My goodness," Natalie replied, a little flustered. "Have you lost weight? I'm sorry. That's a rude thing to ask—"

"No! No! I'm so glad you noticed. I've lost thirty pounds since the end of summer."

"Thirty pounds! Wow, that's fantastic! I'm sure that was hard."

"Yeah. A lot of salads—and a lot of treadmill."

Natalie laughed.

"So! Are you coming back to school here?" Jake asked.

And Natalie forgot for a moment that she was blind and holding a cane in her hands and trying to live scared at home. She wanted to say "Yes!" but what she mumbled weakly was "I—I don't know. I was just talking about it with Mrs. Russell."

Jake's voice became serious. "Yeah. Meredith told me a couple weeks ago. About your eyes, I mean."

"It's okay to say the word 'blind,'" Natalie blurted. God, she hoped it didn't sound hostile. She certainly didn't want to drive him away.

"Oh," he responded. "Okay. I'm sorry, Natalie . . . that you're blind. I really am sorry."

She smiled slightly. "But *don't be*, okay?" she coaxed gently. "I don't want anyone to feel sorry for me."

A pause. What Natalie would have given then to be able to see Jake's face.

"Well, if you ask me, it looks like you're doing great," Jake said. He touched her hand, then squeezed it and held it for a few seconds before letting go. "And I do hope you come back, Nat. I need to tell you all about the national convention in Omaha. It was so awesome. And do you know we never even had a special election to pick your replacement? So you could still be on the student council! And, hey, look, can I talk to you about that panel we were going to do? The one with the special needs kids? I think I've talked them into doing it again, but it would be great if you could be there, too."

Jake plunged forward like a high-speed train. Once he got going there was no stopping him. "We could talk to you, too, Natalie. You know, like what were the hurdles? What did you have to overcome? And then maybe—what can we do to help you? Now that you might be coming back."

What did you have to overcome? Despite Jake's warm and encouraging words, Natalie knew she was not ready to return to Western Allegany High School and talk to the students about what it was like to be blind. She wasn't ready because she hadn't overcome the hurdles! What's more, she wasn't sure she could ever overcome them.

"Hey! Now that I know you're home," Jake went on, "could I call you sometime and talk about it?"

"Sure," Natalie quickly agreed, hoping that would stop him. "That would be fine, Jake. Call and we'll talk about it."

And suddenly, Natalie's mother was there. Or had she been there?

"Mrs. O'Reilly. Nice to see you," Jake said.

"And you, Jake," Natalie's mother replied. "You look great!"

Quick good-byes. A walk back through the hall. Was Jake watching as she used her cane? Outside to the car. Door shut. Seat belt on. Safe again. Natalie heaved a sigh of relief and swallowed hard.

Yikes. How scary to think of actually returning to the high school and facing the other kids. By the time Jake called, she figured, she would have thought of some way to get out of it.

But gosh, that hug felt good, she thought, pressing her lips together to stifle the secret smile and the flip-flop feeling in her stomach. And the little hand squeeze? Did her mom notice?

Sitting on the barn step the next morning, holding out crust for the cat to eat, Natalie was besieged by mixed emotions. She wondered if someday she would actually be strong enough to tell the students at her high school what it was like to lose her sight. What *were* the hurdles? And what exactly would she say?

Natalie tried to envision this future scenario because she knew that she wanted it to happen. She would take the microphone and, with confidence, repeat Miss Karen's comment the morning Natalie discovered her sight was gone: *Acknowledge the loss, but don't stay there.* It was important advice, even though she hadn't taken it to heart. Not yet anyway.

The cat nearby meowed, and Natalie removed her glove to see if there was any food left, but the pie tin was empty. "All gone," she said.

And oddly, a snapshot memory of Sheldon appeared in her mind. She saw him at the blackboard, moving his head around so he could see the letters of that English sonnet written in chalk. Curious, the way in which he perceived the world, piecemeal, never able to see—immediately and directly—the all-important center. He had to work at putting things together, always starting from the edges and slowly working his way in. . . .

Suddenly, Natalie jumped, frightened by the strange sensation beneath her fingers. She pulled her hand away and held it to her chest. What in the world? Her heart skipped a beat as something pressed against her arm. Was someone there?! Natalie sucked in her breath—then a slight smile sprouted as she realized it was the cat.

The cat was purring. Natalie could hear and feel the vibrations. Slowly, she reached out and petted the animal's soft, furry head until her fingers discovered a rough, crusty spot. Was he missing an ear? The cat pulled back and ran away.

"Hey! I'm going to have to give you a name!" Natalie called after him.

"DO WHAT YOU HAVE TO DO"

After dinner the next evening, Natalie's father made a fire in the fireplace. For a few moments, Natalie simply sat by it, enjoying the warmth and the popping, crackling sound of the burning oak logs. She had the cell phone in her hand. It was time, she had decided, as she pressed speed dial "6" for Meredith.

Meredith: *Hey—why didn't you call me? I didn't know you were home until we saw your mom at the grocery store. When do you go back?*

Natalie: *Don't know that I am.*

Meredith: *Really? Are you coming back to school then?*

Natalie: *Maybe.*

Natalie was relieved Meredith didn't press the issue.

Meredith: *Well, anyway, I wanted to see you, Nat, before Christmas. I wanted to apologize for the crummy way I acted at Thanksgiving. Seems like I keep apologizing to you.*

Natalie: *It's been hard. What we're both going through is pretty hard.*

Meredith: *Hard for me? Natalie, you're the one who lost her sight!*

Natalie: *True. But you're the one who has to deal with a blind friend now.*

Silence.

Meredith: *I have a Christmas present for you. Can I bring it over tomorrow? Like what are you doing tomorrow night?*

Natalie: *My parents are going out. One of those firehouse dinners. I'm staying home to babysit Nuisance, who is due to deliver any day.*

Meredith: *Do you need help babysitting your goat? I mean, we don't have to deliver babies or anything, do we?*

Natalie (laughing): *I hope not! If Nuisance goes into labor, I'd call my mom and dad. And yeah, sure, it would be great for you to come. . . .*

All the next day, Natalie looked forward to having Meredith over. Another phone call between the two confirmed plans for turning the evening into a sleepover. Natalie wrapped a pair of gloves and some hand lotion as gifts, and planned out snacks and drinks with her mother.

Meredith, who now had her learner's permit, drove over to Natalie's house that night, and then said good-bye to her father.

"Wow. Mom says you drove over," Natalie said.

"Yeah," Meredith said as she came through the front door. Natalie heard the crinkle of a shopping bag.

"I'll probably have my license by summer," she said. "Once I can drive myself, then we can go shopping, or down to the lake whenever we want. Whenever I can get the car, that is."

Natalie reached out to touch her friend, and her hand brushed the bed pillow Meredith always brought with her on sleepovers. Meredith dropped the pillow and gave Natalie a hug. "Come on in," Natalie urged. "I have something for you."

In the living room they sat on the couch.

"It's not much," Natalie warned, handing Meredith a wrapped box.

But Meredith said she loved the gloves and the lotion.

"And yours," Meredith said, handing Natalie a shoe box–size gift.

"Tell me what it looks like first," Natalie said. "The package."

"Oh. Well, it's shiny green paper with sparkly white snowflakes, and there's a red ribbon with a bow my mom tied 'cause she's good at bows."

Natalie grinned and then unwrapped the package. Inside the big box was a smaller box. And inside the smaller box was a slick gift card.

"It's for the mall," Meredith explained. "Twenty-five dollars to spend anywhere. You're going with me, and this time . . . well, I would be proud to walk with you if you use your cane."

Natalie was touched. "You're sure?"

"Absolutely sure. I mean, you need to be using it anyway and getting some practice in, right?"

Natalie's throat grew tight. "Thanks," she told Meredith.

It was cold in the barn, much colder than Natalie had thought. She was glad she had changed into a warmer coat at the last minute. The girls' footsteps echoed, but for only a moment. As soon as the goats caught sight of them, they became excited and a rousing chorus of *waaaahhhhh* began. Natalie used her cane to follow the wall to the second pen on the right, where Nuisance stayed. She unlatched the door and the two girls entered the hay-strewn enclosure.

"Look at her!" squealed Meredith. "She is really pregnant!"

Natalie took one of Meredith's hands and guided it along one of the goat's large, bulging sides. Somehow though, it didn't feel the same. "Dad?"

"I'm here," he said. "I'm right behind you. It feels different, Natty Bean, because she's getting ready to deliver. The baby has moved up into the birth canal. Remember? That's how you tell when she's getting ready to deliver—the belly gets smaller and the bag gets bigger."

Natalie smiled. "Oh, my gosh. My baby is going to have a baby!"

There was a flurry of activity in the barn hallway as Natalie's dad set up a card table for the girls and plugged in a portable heater. Natalie's mother was there, too, arranging bowls of hummus, carrot sticks, corn chips, and peanut M&M's, as well as a thermos of hot chocolate, all the snacks Natalie had requested.

"We're leaving now," her father said. "You know what to do in an emergency, but if you think she's on the brink, give us a call."

"We're all set," Natalie assured him.

She turned to Meredith. "I have a surprise, too," she said. "Look. A whole deck of cards with Braillables."

"What's that?" Meredith asked.

"Little Braille labels that stick on. I made these at school."

"Cool! You mean we can play cards?"

Natalie grinned. And Nuisance whined. "She's been complaining all day," Natalie said. "I'll have to keep giving her back rubs. She's so spoiled. Here, you deal out the cards, Meres. A game of gin rummy?"

A door slammed and they heard Natalie's parents drive away. Natalie was so glad Meredith had come. The girls sat down at the card table and explored the tray of snacks.

"I love your mother's hummus," Meredith said. She used a carrot stick to dip; Natalie heard the crunch.

Nuisance was still moaning. "Listen to her. She sounds so pathetic," Natalie said. She ducked back into the pen and gave Nuisance a quick back rub, then returned to the card table.

"I'm still not very quick with the Braille," Natalie warned, taking her seat again. "So it may take a minute for me to figure out what's here."

"That's okay. Take your time."

A moment passed.

"Nat, aren't you going to pick up your cards and study them?"

"Oh! I didn't know you had already dealt them."

"Yeah, they're right there."

"Where?"

"Right in front of you!"

"Oh. I never heard you deal."

A sigh from Meredith. "I'm sorry. I keep forgetting you can't see."

Natalie found the cards, fanned them out in her hands, and started touching the Braille labels. "I'm glad you forget," she said.

While they played cards, they talked. Natalie told Meredith about running into Jake at school (although Natalie kept the part about him squeezing her hand to herself) and the whole story of what had happened with Bree at school. Meredith, in turn, talked about school and Richie.

"Hey, and so who is this boy at the school in Baltimore who calls?" Meredith asked. "What did you say his name was?"

"Arnab. He's cute. I was able to see him before I lost my vision. He's completely blind. And very smart. So interested in science. Like our last conversation, he wanted to know all the steps we take to make cheese."

"How romantic!" Meredith quipped.

"I know. So there I am telling him about rennet and how it makes the milk separate into curds and whey, and we both crack up and start reciting that Mother Goose thing. You know, Little Miss Muffet sat on a tuffet, eating her—"

"CURDS AND WHEY!" the girls chimed together.

It was right then—as they laughed about "curds and whey"— that a bone-chilling shriek split the night air.

Both Natalie and Meredith nearly dropped the cards in their hands.

"What in the heck is that?" Meredith asked.

"Winston!" Natalie said, sitting up stiffly. "He only does that when there's something prowling around."

"You're kidding, right?"

Winston's shrill noise tore through the night again.

"There's something out there," Natalie said. "A dog or a fox—"

"A bear?" Meredith asked. "Could it be a bear?"

"I guess it's possible," Natalie admitted, recalling what her father had said about bears not hibernating when food was available. "But it's not likely," she added, not wanting to scare Meredith.

"The goats are in, right?" Meredith asked. "And Winston?"

"Yeah, they're all in. Winston's in the back there."

"Then everyone's safe?" Meredith asked.

A loud *whap* at the barn's back doors interrupted them.

"Holy smokes!" Meredith cried.

The heavy barn doors that hung on iron runners swung out and back, crashing against the side of the barn.

The girls froze.

When they heard a loud grunt outside, Meredith screamed and

jumped up from her seat. "It is a bear! Nat, I see him through the window!"

Natalie patted the pockets in her jacket, then her jeans. The cell phone wasn't there!

"Nat, call somebody! Quick!"

Natalie kept checking her pockets and suddenly remembered she'd changed jackets just before coming out. "Shoot! It's back in the kitchen!"

"Oh, no!"

"Let's go lock ourselves in the creamery!" Meredith said, grabbing Natalie's arm.

"It's locked," Natalie said. "We always lock it at the end of the day."

Meredith ran to check the door anyway while the bear rattled the back doors again. The goats bleated in alarm.

Natalie put her hands up to her temples, thinking.

"My dad has a gun," she said, dropping her hands. "Can you use a shotgun?"

"No! Are you kidding me? I don't know what to do with a gun!"

"Well, you're gonna have to learn fast."

Natalie opened her cane and made her way quickly to the grain bin off the main barn hallway several yards away. She dropped the cane on the floor and reached up overhead to where her father had said he would hide the weapon. She needed both hands to lift the heavy shotgun down.

Pressing the safety, she broke open the gun and felt inside the barrels for the shells. The chambers were empty. The gun wasn't loaded.

"Nat, hurry up! The bear is pushing the back door! If he slides it open, he'll come in! Maybe we can climb up into the loft!"

"But the bear will climb up, too!"

"So what do we do?"

On her toes, Natalie reached above the grain bin and felt around the shelf. Spiderwebs, paint chips, old nails—yes! A box of shells. She grabbed the box, unloaded two shells, and dropped them, one at a time, into the chambers. She snapped the gun shut with a forceful, metallic sound, and again put the safety on. She'd forgotten how heavy the gun was.

"Nat, I don't hear him anymore," Meredith said, touching Natalie's arm. "Maybe we should make a run for the house?"

"But what if he's out there?" Natalie asked.

"Yeah. Oh, my gosh."

The goats were on edge now, bleating and moving about in their pens. Natalie could hear their excited hooves against the walls.

"Let's check Nuisance," Natalie said. "Listen to her. She's making a really weird noise. Where are you, Meredith?"

"Here, right in front of you."

"Take the gun," Natalie told her. "It's loaded. If that bear comes in, you need to aim and fire." She felt for the safety on the gun. "Here, let me undo the safety. Careful now—that gun is ready. Don't point it at me!"

"Wow, it's heavy," Meredith said, taking the weapon.

"I know, but you can do it. Just put the stock against your shoulder." She patted the wooden end of the gun. "Aim with the bead at the end of the barrel. It has a big kick, but if you aim right, one shot ought to do it."

"One shot?"

"It's a shotgun, Meredith. A whole bunch of pellets will fly out."

For a full minute or so, they stood still, listening. The goats were still agitated and bleating, but the back door was still. Natalie picked up her cane. "Let's get back. I need to check Nuisance."

"What do I do with this gun?" Meredith asked.

"Put the safety back on and leave it on the table."

It was still quiet. Thank God, Natalie thought. She hoped the bear had moved on.

In the pen, Nuisance was lying down, breathing rapidly. Natalie kneeled down and ran her hands along the goat's side and felt a moistness at tail's end. "Meredith, she's having her baby!"

"Oh, great! So now we have a bear at the door and a goat having a baby! What do we do?"

"Nothing, I hope. Calm down, Meres. She should be okay. I just need to be here in case something goes wrong."

Natalie desperately hoped the bear had gone, although she was aware it might be lured back by the smells of birth.

Nuisance groaned.

"The baby's coming out!" Meredith shouted with alarm.

Natalie reached into the corner of the pen, where they had stacked a pile of clean towels, and grabbed one. Then she kneeled again beside Nuisance. "Take it easy, babe," she murmured, trying to soothe the goat.

Nuisance kept groaning. Natalie could tell she was pushing. But why was this baby taking so long? Was something wrong? Natalie reached down and felt a warm liquid. Was it normal? Was it blood? Then she felt one leg, not two, coming out of the mother.

"Oh, no," Natalie moaned. This meant the other leg was stuck inside. If her father were here, he'd reach inside the goat right now, find the other leg, and guide it out. If the leg wasn't freed, it could tear up the mother's insides, making her hemorrhage and bleed to death! Like Daisy, she thought, panic gripping her as she flashed back to that terrible night six years ago and the pool of blood when Nuisance was born. It couldn't happen again, could it? No! She did not want Nuisance—or her baby—to die.

Natalie whipped off her coat and pushed her right sleeve back above her elbow. Her dad always took off his wedding ring when he had to do this so it didn't catch on anything. Quickly, Natalie pulled the pearl ring off her right finger and shoved it deep inside the pocket of her jeans.

"What are you going to do?" Meredith asked.

"One leg is caught," Natalie replied. Then, taking a full breath, Natalie wiggled her hand in—then her arm—trying to follow the kid's slimy, protruding leg. It was wet and warm inside the goat. Natalie did not want to think about it. She just wanted to get in there and find the other leg.

Suddenly, there was a solid *thump*! against the back doors.

"Nat, the bear's back! He's banging the door! What do I do?"

"Meredith, I can't help you! Get the gun. If he comes in, fire!"

Meredith left the pen. Natalie heard the latch click.

Another loud smashing sound at the back doors. The bear was throwing his full weight against it.

"Natalie! I'm scared! I can't do this! Let's hide in the loft!"

"Meredith, I can't see! You can climb up there—or you can do what you have to do and help me!"

Even then, even in the frenzy of that moment, those words resonated with meaning. But there was no time to dwell on it.

Natalie had to concentrate on what she was feeling because she was inside Nuisance up to her elbow. Even eyesight wouldn't help her now. She was groping in the darkness. All at once her fingers felt a little hoof. One tiny, little hoof. She ran her fingers along the leg until she had a grip, then carefully pushed it back and straightened it against the other leg. Slowly, keeping a grip on both feet, she pulled her arm back.

Meredith screamed. "It's trying to open the doors!"

"Pop the safety and get your aim up!"

"I can't do this!" Meredith cried.

Gently, Natalie tugged on the baby goat's legs. When her arm was out again, she let Nuisance do the rest, and within seconds a small, slimy goat slid out into Natalie's waiting hands. She laid it on the ground and waited for Nuisance to turn and lick her new baby. Seven big licks and she'd have it cleaned off. Then she'd nudge the baby to stand up.

Things were quiet again. Relieved, Natalie stood up and wiped her arm and hands with a towel. "You okay, Meres? She asked.

No answer. Had she gone up into the loft?

The silence was unsettling. Even the goats were quiet.

"Meredith?" she called urgently. "Are you there?"

Still no answer.

Suddenly, the sound of breaking glass and a horrible, heavy crash.

A shotgun blast filled the air and Natalie dropped to her knees.

TEEN SHOOTS BEAR

HAWLEY—A 15-year-old girl shot and killed a 150-pound black sow last night as the bear threatened her, a friend, and 80 goats in a barn at Mountainside Farm.

Meredith Keefer, 15, and Natalie O'Reilly, 14, daughter of farm owners Frank and Jean O'Reilly, were tending a goat about to give birth when the bear showed up at the barn's back doors and started lunging against the building.

"Our llama, Winston, gave us the heads-up," said Miss O'Reilly, who is blind. "But we had no idea what was out there. Then Meredith actually saw the bear through the window."

Neither one had immediate access to a phone to call for help. Moving quickly, Miss O'Reilly found the shotgun her father had stored in the barn for protection and loaded two shells into the chambers. "I hunted with my dad when I was younger," she explained. "So it was no big deal."

But firing the gun was impossible for Miss O'Reilly, who recently lost her sight due to glaucoma. "I told Meredith she had to do it."

It was a first for Miss Keefer. "I watched my brother shoot clay pigeons once, so I had an idea of how to hold a gun, but I never fired one. Natty told me to just aim and fire. When that bear started coming in, that's what I did. I popped the safety. I aimed. And I fired. I saw the bear fall, but I could tell it wasn't dead. I fired a second time to be sure."

Meanwhile, Miss O'Reilly helped to deliver triplets to her pet goat, Nuisance. "The first baby was stuck and I had to help a little. But after that, Nuisance did all the work."

The Department of Natural Resources police took the bear and will perform tests to determine if the animal had rabies, which would explain its aggressive behavior. "A rabid bear is unusual, but not unheard of out here," said Kevin Smith, a biologist with the department. "It's entirely possible if the bear has come in contact with a species that normally carries rabies, such as a raccoon, a bat, or a skunk."

Neither Miss Keefer nor Miss O'Reilly will have to have post-exposure rabies vaccinations, because neither one of them touched the animal or came into contact with its blood.

"All in all, it was a pretty exciting evening," said Miss Keefer. "I mean, it sure beat the game of gin rummy we were playing."

FROM NOW ON

Natalie loved listening to her mother read the article from the Oakland newspaper. There were more interviews, too; three other reporters called and one came out to the house. There was even a television spot in the barn with lights set up and cables running all over the place. The goats went nuts with excitement. Meredith said they were climbing over one another to watch.

"You are truly an amazing person!" the television reporter gushed to Natalie. "Loading that gun and delivering goats even though you're blind!"

"No!" Natalie protested, almost laughing. "No, I am *not* an amazing person. Please don't write that. I'm a girl who grew up on a goat farm, and I know about guns because I once hunted with my father. It just so happens that I am blind, too."

Natalie turned to where she knew Meredith stood beside her. "Meredith is the one who's amazing, because she had never fired a shotgun before!"

Behind both of them stood Natalie's father, who had a hand on each of their shoulders. "I couldn't be more proud of these girls."

Part of Natalie was actually sad for the bear, which turned out to have had rabies. It was just a living creature, she thought, who happened to get sick. But the shooting and the births—life and death at the same time—had marked a turning point for her. She knew that if she could do what she had to do that night, she could do just about anything.

But no more deals with God, she decided as she rode the bus back to the school in Baltimore on a frigid Sunday afternoon in mid-January. From now on she would put aside the anger, the doubt, and all the regrets, and just try to move forward.

Good memories from her extended holiday break kept her warm on the cold, bumpy ride back to Baltimore: the time spent with Meredith at the mall picking out fuzzy socks and earrings, and her new friend, a furry, one-eared cat she had named Oliver (for Oliver Twist, the Charles Dickens character who also lived through hard times). Not to mention the three kids, which Natalie's mother said looked just like Nuisance. Natalie named the two little does Hunky and Dory, and called the feisty young buck Mr. Lee. And then, of course, she recalled the moments spent with Jake in her own living room, talking about school and what she had yet to learn, and how they might finally be together again on the student council, perhaps as early as next year, but probably not until senior year.

"But I think we ought to get together this summer to start planning," he told Natalie. He touched her hand again, only this time he held it for a moment and even played with her pearl ring. Natalie's heart beat double time.

"As soon as I learn JAWS, I'll e-mail," she promised.

Natalie felt on the bus seat beside her to be sure she had her new cane, already identified with the whistle from her old cane. She touched her backpack, too. There was a small, refrigerated pack of goat cheese for Arnab, and a tin of chocolate chip cookies she had made to share in the dorm. There was her completed essay on gun control, which she had carefully Brailled out, and, attached to the essay, a newspaper clipping. Also in her backpack was a note from Miss Audra with a date on it—a date for when they would visit the Baltimore City Jail to try to make a voice identification of the two men who had attacked Natalie and Bree. Miss Audra said that in addition to assault, there was now talk of charging the men with manslaughter, or possibly second-degree murder.

There would be no punishment from the school for leaving the campus without permission. Natalie had suffered enough, they said. The only apprehension Natalie had about returning to school was moving back into a room that would be so empty without Bree. Of course, that was not the only empty spot Bree had left behind.

The thing was, if you wanted to survive you had to keep going, Natalie had decided. Even when it hurt. Sometimes, she had discovered, you had to walk around the holes in your life, instead of falling into them.

By late April, the sun had melted the last, stubborn patches of ice and snow in western Maryland. The slowly warming land yielded a host of sensory pleasures, including a new symphony of birdsongs and the earthy smell of freshly sprouted plants and soft mud. The sun's warm rays were welcome in the clear, crisp mountain air.

"I think it's great that you're taking time out of your spring break for a tour of the university," Professor Brodsky said. "It's good to start looking at colleges your sophomore year in high school when the pressure is off. Before you leave, Natalie, be sure I give you that paperwork for the internship next year, okay?"

He rubbed his hands together. "All right then. I've got two college students here, Nathan and Gillian, who will help out this morning. I thought we'd tour Frostburg's library first, and then visit some classrooms, the dining hall, and finally, the dorms. Do any of you have questions?"

"Not yet," said Serena. "But I'm staying at Natalie's farm the rest of this week—we're going to learn how to make cheese! Yeah. How cool is that? But if we come up with a question, can we e-mail?"

"Of course," the professor replied.

"Actually, I do have one question," Natalie said. "Do we still call you professor even though you're a state senator now?"

He laughed. "Professor is fine."

Eve raised her hand to ask something, too. "I just wondered if, in the dorms, can three people room together?"

"I'm in a triple now," Gillian, the tour guide, told them. "If you ask me, we have more space than in a double."

"Some accommodations can be made," the professor said, "because we are all hoping this will work out."

Hope, yes, Natalie thought to herself. There was always hope, wasn't there? Only now, she realized, she didn't need a stone in her pocket to have it. She would never stop hoping for her sight to return. Who knew what scientific research might uncover for the blind?

In the meantime, Natalie kept reminding herself, unless you wanted to fold up and die, or go home to live scared, you simply kept going—in a forward direction. Life could still be good. Very good.

Professor Brodsky was waiting, and holding the door open. "Well," he said, "let's get started."

Braille Alphabet

The six dots of
the braille cell are
arranged and numbered:

$$
\begin{array}{ccc}
1 & \bullet\ \bullet & 4 \\
2 & \bullet\ \bullet & 5 \\
3 & \bullet\ \bullet & 6
\end{array}
$$

The capital sign, dot 6,
placed before a letter
makes a capital letter.

$$
\begin{array}{ccc}
1 & & 4 \\
2 & & 5 \\
3 & \bullet & 6
\end{array}
$$

The number sign, dots 3, 4, 5, 6,
placed before the characters
a through j, makes the numbers
1 through 0. For example: <u>a</u> preceded
by the number sign is 1, <u>b</u> is 2, etc.

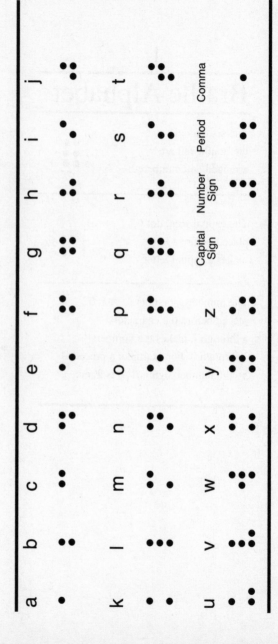

PRAISE FOR *RED KAYAK*

"With this finely crafted novel, Cummings . . . firmly establishes herself as an outstanding writer for early teens. The writing here is direct and clear; the setting, characterizations, and voices ring with authenticity; the situation is tense and the stakes high."   —*VOYA*

"This well-crafted story will have broad appeal."
                                        —*School Library Journal*

"A memorable story . . . each character is believable . . . there is plenty of action to appeal to readers."   —*KLIATT*

"[A] well-written, sometimes gripping story."
                                               —*Kirkus Reviews*

Turn the page for a preview of another
gripping story by Priscilla Cummings . . .

RED KAYAK

CHAPTER ONE

After all this time, I still ask myself: *Was it my fault?*
Maybe. Maybe not.

Either way, I wonder what would have happened if
I'd called out a warning. Or kept my mouth shut later.
Would J.T. and Digger still be my best friends? Would the
DiAngelos still be living next door?

One thing's for sure: If none of this had happened, I'd be
out there crabbing every day, baiting my pots in the morning and pulling them in after school. Fall's a great time for
catching crabs before the females head south and the males
burrow into the mud. I could fix the engine on the boat
easy if I wanted. It's not broken like I told Dad. Probably
nothing but some air in the lines from settin' there so long.
I could bleed the engine tonight, set my alarm for 4 A.M.,
and be on the river before the sun was up over the tree line.

Don't think it didn't bother me, the way those traps sat
all summer, stacked four deep against the back of Dad's
toolshed. Some never even got hosed off, they were stashed

in such a hurry. Be a lot of work to clean 'em up and re-zinc them, too, so they don't corrode. In just a few days, though, I could have four rows of twenty-five sunken pots out there, each one marked with a fresh-painted orange buoy, and all one hundred of those pots soaked and baited with razor clams. Afternoons, I could be hauling in crabs hand over fist, and right now, a bushel of big number-one jimmies would fetch me seventy dollars from the whole-saler—maybe even more, since the price of crabs has gone through the roof.

But this is all so complicated. I can't go back out on the water. Not yet anyway. I can't help it; I keep asking myself, *What if this, what if that?* And then in my mind I see that red kayak . . .

My dad says stop thinking that way. "You be lookin' back-ward all the time, Brady, you're gonna have one heck of a crook in the neck." He smiles when he says that. But I know what he means deep down, and it's not funny. You can't keep dwelling on the past when you can't undo it. You can't make it happen any different than it did.

My cousin Carl comes over a lot. He's a paramedic and sees a lot of gross stuff, so he knows about getting things out of your head. "Talk it out there, boy," he keeps telling me. "What? You think you're alone? You think other people don't have these feelings?" But even Carl admits he's never been in quite the same position as me.

Mom has helped a lot, too, although I know it was really hard for her, because of my sister.

Mostly, I wish I could just stop going over it in my mind.

But it replays all the time. Like waves breaking on the narrow beach down at the river. Sometimes, after school, I walk down there to sit on the bank and do nothing. Just let the sun bake my face and listen to those waves hitting the shore, one after the other.

Tilly always follows me and I let her. Tilly's my yellow Lab. She lays down with her head on her paws and knows to leave me alone when I'm thinking. Despite everything, I still marvel at how all those tiny ripples in the water can catch the sunlight and make the river shimmer like a million jewels were strewn on the surface. Deceptive, how other times the same water can seem as smooth as glass. You'd never know that underneath, the currents run so hard and so fast.

It's a pretty river, the Corsica. But it doesn't have a heart . . .

CHAPTER TWO

In some ways, it started over a year ago. But I want to get the worst over first, so I'm going to start with what happened six months ago, in the spring. That morning, we were waiting, my two friends and I, for the ambulance to come, and J.T. took a swig from his bottle of green tea. I remember this because Digger was trying to pick a fight, and it all started with J.T.'s green tea.

No one was hurt—that's not why the ambulance was coming. My cousin Carl had this old ambulance that the county still uses for a backup, and when he had the early shift, he would swing by and give us a ride to school. School's only a couple miles away, but it's a forty-minute ride on that dang bus because we're first pickup on the loop. Besides, it was pretty cool getting a ride in the ambulance.

J.T. almost always waits for the bus with me. He lives next door on his family's chicken farm. A soybean field between my house and his has a path worn down through the middle of it we're back and forth so much. And Digger is across the road, not too far the other way. Sometimes, he walks over to join us—that, or his father will drop him off from his dump truck on his way to a job.

So we were in the driveway that morning, waiting for Carl to pick us up. Backpacks on the ground. Hunched in our parkas because it was chilly. Taking turns throwing the tennis ball for Tilly, who never quits. And Digger snatched the bottle of green tea out of J.T.'s hands and started laughing. "What the—"

"Shhhhh!" I'm always having to tone down Digger. "My mom can hear!" And she can't stand to hear us cuss.

We cast a glance back at the house.

Digger held the bottle up, out of J.T.'s reach. "Green tea with ginseng and *honey*?" He sounded disgusted.

It made me uncomfortable, the way Digger talked to J.T. sometimes. And after all those years we spent growing up together.

But J.T. just laughed. He's pretty easygoing. And he swiped the drink back. "Hey," he said. "It's loaded with antioxidants."

"Anti *who*?" Digger screwed up his face.

"You wait, Digger," J.T. warned him. "You and Brady—especially Brady 'cause he's always out in the sun—you'll be all old and wrinkly by the time you're fifty, and I'll have, like, this perfect skin."

"Yeah, like a baby's ass," Digger retorted.

I wanted to tell him to shut up, but I didn't. I could tell when Digger was in one of his moods.

"You're just jealous," J.T. quipped.

"Of *what*?" Digger demanded.

"Guys!" I called out, stopping everything like a referee's whistle. When they looked at me, I pivoted and flung the ball for Tilly. We watched it land and roll downhill toward our dock. At the same time my father's band saw started up in the old tractor shed, which Dad has transformed into his woodworking shop. Where we live used to be a farm, but it's not anymore. The barn and the farmhouse burned down years ago—before my parents bought the property and built a one-story brick rancher. My dad is a waterman half the year, a boat carpenter the other half, and even though crabbing season started April 1, he'd been working Mondays in the shop because he was making more money building cabinets than crabbing, especially now that crabs were getting scarce.

Last year, the state legislature cut Dad's workday from fourteen hours down to eight. Then the governor took away the month of November, and it hurt us financially. My mom had to put in extra hours at the nursing home, and Dad was pretty ticked off. "They're blamin' the wrong people!" he railed. "Pollution and development—that's what's killin' us. Bay be right smart of crabs if it weren't for all the damned condo-*minions* going up!"

I don't know. We had a little argument about it after a scientist came to school. He said my dad was only half right—about the pollution and all. "We're fishing the bay too hard," that guy kept saying. "Too many crab pots, too many trotlines. You have to take the long look."

When Dad's noisy band saw stopped, I glanced at J.T. and Digger and wondered which way the conversation would go.

"What's your dad working on?" J.T. asked.

"Dr. Finney's sailboat," I said, glad to move off the subject of J.T.'s green tea. "Thirty-foot Seawind ketch. Twenty-five years old—fiberglass hull but a lot of solid wood trim topside."

J.T. arched his eyebrows. "Wow. He's got his work cut out for him."

"He's completely gutting it," I said. "Dr. Finney's going to put in this incredible electronics system. GPS. Flat-screen TV. Security." I knew this would make J.T. drool because he loves all that technical stuff.

But it only made Digger angry. He kicked a rock in the driveway. "Some people got too much money for their own damn good."

When a pair of noisy mallards flew over, we looked up. Even Tilly dropped the ball and started barking. In the west, I noticed dark clouds piling up across the horizon, like a distant mountain range.

"If the weather didn't look so bad, I'd say come on over this afternoon. We could take a little spin down the river." I felt bad for Digger sometimes. On account of his family.

"Can't go," he mumbled, still kicking his toe in the dirt. "I gotta help my old man haul gravel."

"Yeah, me neither," J.T. said. "I erased my entire hard drive last night. I need to load everything back on and rewrite that essay for English. Hey, Brady, remember those oxymorons we talked about in lit the other day?"

"Jumbo shrimp?" I asked.

"Yeah—and *military intelligence*," J.T. reminded me.

I grinned.

"Well, I got a good one for you," J.T. said. *"Microsoft Works."*

Even Digger lifted his head and chuckled. "A *perfect idiot,*" he added.

So there we were, all of us laughing because we'd knocked out four oxymorons smack in a row—and that's when we first saw the red kayak.

From where we stood, you could see down the grassy slope behind our house, on past Dad's shop and the dock, to the creek. And out there, heading our way, was Mr. DiAngelo's new red kayak.

Digger's face lit up. "The Italian stallion," he chortled, a dual reference to the heritage of our new neighbor, Marcellus DiAngelo, and his obsession with physical fitness. Cupping his hands around his mouth, Digger pretended to call out: "Paddle hard, you sucker!"

He and J.T. exchanged this look I didn't quite catch, and J.T. started laughing, too.

But I shook my head. "He shouldn't be going out there today. When he gets down by the point—he'll *fly* down the river." I was sure Mr. DiAngelo didn't know about how the wind picked up once you left our creek and hit the open water. Not to mention the spring tides. Sometimes they were so strong they'd suck the crab-pot buoys under. I doubted whether Mr. DiAngelo knew that; he'd only had the kayak a few weeks.

"Really, guys. We ought to yell something," I said soberly.

J.T. shook his head. "He's too far away. He won't hear you."

"Why should we anyway?" Digger asked with a scowl. "Just

because you baby-sat for their little kid and you're in love with his wife?"

An overstatement if I ever heard one. Although I did take care of their son one afternoon when Mrs. DiAngelo had to go over the bridge to Annapolis for a doctor's appointment. And she is a very good-looking woman—but even J.T. and Digger thought so.

"Ben's cool," I said, trying to make light of it. "We did LEGOs."

J.T. chuckled and looked at his sneakers.

Sneering, Digger stuffed his hands in his pockets. "Look, Brady," he said, "if he's stupid enough to be out there today, he can take what's coming. Besides, he deserves it."

Tilly whined because she was waiting for me to throw the ball again.

"That water is damn cold," I said as I stooped to pick up the ball. It was only the middle of April, and the water temperature probably wasn't even fifty degrees yet. "Exposure, you know? If he fell in, he could die in, like, twenty minutes."

Digger smiled. "Exactly," he said calmly. "We'd all be so lucky."

At that point, I threw the ball so hard it landed in the marsh near the water. Tilly took off after it like a shot and disappeared into the tall grass.

"Come on." I made eye contact with Digger when I said it again: "Let's yell something."

But we didn't.

Digger dropped his eyes and backed off. When he turned in profile, I glimpsed the hard lines of his scowl as he gazed out toward that red kayak. It was the first time I realized how much anger Digger had packed inside. I knew he was sore because the DiAngelos bought his grandfather's farm, tore down the old house, and built a mansion up there on the bluff. But up until then, maybe I hadn't realized how much it bothered him.

Of course it didn't help that we'd all been booted off the property a few days ago. But if you asked me, Mr. DiAngelo was pretty nice about it. He didn't yell, or offend us, or anything like that. He merely asked us to leave because we were trespassing. And Digger *did* have that cigarette lit. I mean, Mr. DiAngelo had a right. For all he knew, we could have started a fire or something.

But from Digger's point of view, we were only hanging out under *our* cliff, where we hung out a million times over the last thirteen years. That cliff and all the property the DiAngelos now own was all part of our stomping grounds. We shot tin cans out on the cornfield. Built forts in the woods. Raced go-carts down the tractor roads. So you know, I *did* feel for some of Digger's frustration.

What I don't understand is how Digger could have been so callous that morning: *If he's stupid enough to be out there, he can take what's coming* . . . How Digger—and J.T., too—could have been so blind to the awful possibilities. Even after I reminded them: *He could die in, like, twenty minutes . . . We ought to yell something . . .*

When, exactly, did they begin to feel shamed by it?

Because it has always shamed me.

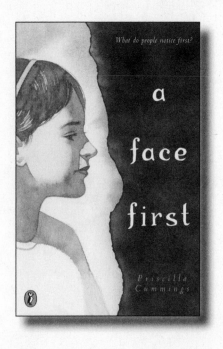

What do people notice first?

a
face
first

Priscilla
Cummings

After a catastrophic automobile accident, twelve-year-old Kelley wakes up to find her face and body severely burned. How will she ever recover and face the world again?